The Unspoken Truth

Angelica Garnett

Chatto & Windus
LONDON

'The Birthday Party' © Angelica Garnett 1990. First p _____ hal Moment,
Angelica Garnett, Puckerbrush Press, Orono, Maine.

Angelica Garnett has asserted her right under the Copyright, Designs
and Patents Act 1988 to be identified as the author of this work.

First published in Great Britain in 2010 by
Chatto & Windus
Random House, 20 Vauxhall Bridge Road,
London SW1V 2SA

www.rbooks.co.uk

Addresses for companies within The Random House Group Limited can be found at:
www.randomhouse.co.uk/offices.htm

The Random House Group Limited Reg. No. 954009

A CIP catalogue record for this book
is available from the British Library

ISBN 9780701184353

The Random House Group Limited supports The Forest Stewardship Council (FSC),
the leading international forest certification organisation. All our titles that are printed
on Greenpeace approved FSC certified paper carry the FSC logo. Our paper procurement
policy can be found at: www.rbooks.co.uk/environment

Mixed Sources
Product group from well-managed
forests and other controlled sources
www.fsc.org Cert no. TT-COC-2139
© 1996 Forest Stewardship Council

FSC

Typeset by Palimpsest Book Production Limited, Grangemouth, Stirlingshire

Printed in the UK by CPI Mackays, Chatham ME5 8TD

CONTENTS

For Henry and Christiane Lewis, in gratitude for their
many acts of kindness

When All The Leaves Were Green, My Love

On one side there was Maman, on the other Nan. They were like the sun and the moon, and she was pulled between. She could feel the strength of the tide in Maman, not to be resisted, the soft haven of her arms, the sweetness of her smile – but in Nan there was something else, less profound, and more reassuring.

Being with Nan was like eating brown bread with the butter scraped on it, wholesome, a little sour, and without excitement. Together they had their own innocent and limited rituals, such as walking down to the high road and counting the cars, picking oak apples and those whorls of pinkish threads called pin cushions, making poppy-dolls, and singing 'John Brown's Body' as they tramped back to the house, and the hundred and one acts of hair-brushing, neck-washing and dos and don'ts that filled the interstices. But when the door opened and Maman came in with a rush of warm air, Bettina ran and hid her face in her skirt, feeling her mother's long fingers caressing the top of her head while Maman said a few words to Nan. The pleasure had become suddenly acute, the choices too many. Another life was waiting for her downstairs, a life that seemed to ride on suave, joyous voices that carried her upwards like a butterfly on the breeze. In them Bettina heard an ease and control, an incipient laughter that she never heard in Nan's voice, and when they descended to her level and included her in the tantalising game they seemed to be playing, she wriggled with a mixture of pleasure and embarrassment. Unlike Nan, the people in the drawing room didn't take her for granted; she was someone special.

But when she came to think of it, those were not the best moments. They were too exciting and churned her up, promising to satisfy, yet never doing so. It was like being in a hall of mirrors, where she saw only reflections of herself. On every face, in every voice there was a smile of special significance, which was trained on her, creating a barrier. No one acknowledged it, or appeared to notice the way in which it invaded her and melted the pride out of her, as though the marrow of Bettina's bones were a mere fluid. If, trying to regain her self-respect, she became sulky and – leaning against Maman's knee – grew as thundrous as she knew how, the voices betrayed alarm, vying with each other in their anxiety to prevent her – from what? From making a scene? What scene could she possibly make, given that it all remained a complete mystery, even to her?

Deep inside Bettina grew the seed of defeatism, a germ sown by no one in particular and, if ever noticed, denied by all. Maman took to soothing Bettina, as though administering whiffs of ether, in an effort to lull her complaints as well as, perhaps, her own misgivings. Bettina knew in advance that if she screamed and hit her heels on the floor, she would only be repaid with smiles and promises, and it was not these she wanted but – as she now saw – simple understanding. It was from Maman that she wanted it most, who seemed the least able to give it.

She could see that, from the giver's point of view, understanding is one of the least simple of things. In Maman's case it would have meant an abdication from the throne she clung to: not only a vision of herself as the dispenser of love, but also as the alpha and omega of Bettina's life, playing a role that, precisely because it was a role, seemed false.

No doubt it had been adopted to hide something: in a confused way, this was evident to Bettina, but it was like being involved in a continuous game of Blind Man's Bluff – however strongly she felt it, she was unable to name it. Even if her feelings constantly betrayed her, they fell on ears that, if not actually deaf, were tuned to another wavelength. Nothing was ever brought to a head, the moment of truth never arrived and her emotions, strong as they seemed, retreated, leaving nothing behind them but dry grit and the impression that she was unutterably stupid. They seemed to atrophy and melt into little blobs of meaninglessness. Maman smothered her so much that she did not know what she wanted, what she could or might have: only that it was something there was never enough of and which maybe no one wanted her to have. In the end there was only a thin white line, like a scar, to remind her of these gulfs of nothing, resembling dark chasms which she had to cross as best she might. And even when Maman was trying to console her, Bettina could not explain what was wrong.

It was true that, all those years ago, Nan had been more reassuring, in an ordinary down-to-earth way – but had she been more trustworthy? On reflection Bettina felt that she had responded to her simply because it was so much easier and simpler. Nan had presented her with a ready-made code, constructed on such a basic level that she could follow it blindfold and – perhaps this was the real point – could merely pay lip service and then escape into her own world of dragons and princesses. Even if Nan was apparently more trustworthy, simply because more predictable, she was, for different reasons, just as manipulative.

In a way you could have said that there was a running battle, or rather an area of total misunderstanding, between Nan and Maman: Maman's noble ideals of civilisation and freedom were subjected to constant erosion by Nan's narrow, potent romanticism, her vision of the Lady of the House, with her little daughter, so touching, so perfect, reflecting with precision all Nan's care in bringing her up in cleanliness and order. All or both: nothing real . . . only permitted by Maman because, however much she thought she disliked it, it saved a lot of trouble.

When Nan said something, Bettina knew she meant what she said, and nothing else. It was dull, but there was at least no need to worry that she hadn't understood. In the world of the drawing room or the studio, however, every word meant at least two things, and the uppermost meaning was the least important. Most things were said as jokes, but there was always a lick at the end like a cat's tongue, which ruffled the petals inside her, and sometimes jerked something out of her which she wished she hadn't said. Like the time she called her father Howard 'obtuse'. It turned out to be such a strong word, so much more concentrated than what she had meant, like a tablespoon of potent medicine. He took it very well of course – he always did – it actually seemed to bounce off him. But she could see, all the same, from the way his pale eyes fluttered, that she had gone too far, and she felt ashamed.

. But in her turn she was often forced to protect herself. Their humour, she learned later, was called irony, and she often didn't care for the laughter that coloured it and, driven to impotent rage, often misunderstood what was beneath it. Sometimes she felt as though they were all against her – and yet they denied it and said she was only being silly, but that was poor comfort. Perhaps she was stupid; little by little a conviction of her limitations possessed her – there was an invisible line beyond which she never went. She stopped where they seemed to think she would remain: a little girl who slotted into a certain place – frilly, diaphanous, nothing serious could be expected of her. She couldn't compete with her brothers, they were so much older, already formed, solid, authoritarian. If they thought she was a nuisance they ordered her to go away. Other things they could share, but she could never be their equal in mind. And so she danced crazily outside their circle, like a fly that wants to get out in winter.

But now, sixty years later, another voice intervenes, low but clear – only too clear. Every word meant at least two things. What is different about that? Don't they always, in all human intercourse? What was it that particularly got under Bettina's skin? Would she have appreciated being brought up entirely, say, by Nan, and have had the advantage of always knowing where she was? Or would it actually have turned out to be a place entirely devoid of interest?

Perhaps she really was without intelligence then; and yet with such a thin skin, and the older generation so much older, their laughter did seem alien – wounding rather than amusing. And the suspicion must have come to her that, while trying to defend themselves from her – an unknown quantity – they were seeking to make her into something they could understand. Bettina, of course, didn't see herself as a threat but somehow, because of her youthfulness and the gap between her world and theirs, inevitably was. And she was stupid, naturally and beautifully stupid, with the gullibility of the young, unable to believe they could be afraid of her. The trouble was that Bettina's good faith wasn't strong enough. It abandoned her, and she allowed herself to become putty in their hands. They meant well – or thought they did – but not well enough to be honestly straightforward with her.

In this sense Bettina was the sole child among them, her only weapons terribly unsophisticated, whereas on their side they had all the advantage of experience, tempting her to see them as an élite into which, one day, she might be invited. Nan's world, good as it was, was put into the shade by the impure pleasures of studio and drawing room, where the rewards were so unreal and ephemeral.

At the same time it was maybe because she was a little girl: she could dance and sing and say the first thing that came into her head, and, laughing, they encouraged her until she was drunk with excitement and pleasure. It was like being on a big dipper and she was the only person who could set it going. Maman was always there to catch her if she fell off, sometimes in tears, especially if it was her father Howard who lost patience with her. Mamam was calm – she built a magic hedge round Bettina or wrapped her in cotton wool.

Then one day Bettina was truly rude to Howard. She didn't know why – it just came out of her like the whip of a snake's tongue. She couldn't actually remember what she had said, but she recalled the feeling – the shock of losing her self-control, and the expression of surprise on Howard's face, the way he'd stopped speaking for a second, and then carried on as though nothing had happened. It was in the park, after the Flower Show. He was going to watch the cricket match and she was on her way home, having wandered round the trestle tables set out in the Riding School and gazed at the huge vegetable marrows and mammoth leeks, at the chocolate cakes and little pieces of embroidery in daisy stitch, turned pale by the ashy light that came through the glass roof. She remembered going home through the long grass, all on her own, unaware of exactly how rude she had been.

Yet Howard, preoccupied with the affairs of the world, reflective yet genial, was always attentive to her. But even he was never more than only half there. He nonetheless generated hot little flames of excitement that made her twirl around like a flower in the sun; he also made her squirm, as though a powerful light were suddenly trained on her out of the dark and there she was, exposed and at his mercy. He had no idea what she felt, or whether she really wanted his affection. Sometimes she did, and then she would get very excited and jump or shout, and smell his tweed and tobacco as he hugged her in an effort to suppress some of her exuberance. As she bounced and twisted she knew he was really feeble, had no authority and had got more than he had bargained for. On the other side of the room Maman smiled painfully – she was caught between Bettina and Howard and had no authority either. Rough little girls were like burrs on the skin – thoroughly uncomfortable.

Soon Nan would come in and stand just inside the door observing – silent and inexorable. Even Howard had to give way to her and was grateful for her interruption. As the door shut Bettina would hear her name mentioned, and the words 'charming, charming'. What did it mean, and why did that word always give her a shivery feeling, so that she could never use it herself? But once the door was shut, she was in a world without surprises, one that she could inhabit blindfold, that she trusted, full of common sense.

In those years the house and the whole of life was bathed in colour: it mottled or streaked the walls and furniture and sang silent but powerful songs from room to room, space to space. In the morning, the pink and yellow curtains drawn across the window mendaciously promising a fine day even when the sky was water-filled, blowing inwards as the breeze explored the room, momentarily filling it with air, and the colours she knew so well answered each other like a game of ping-pong – they glowed and sizzled and almost shrieked with the pleasure – the black, the Indian red, the peacock blue or yellow ochre. She could never think of the house without them: it was as though they had grown there and when, later, she returned year after year, though imperceptibly faded, they rose again and struck their strange chords like a forgotten musical instrument.

As she grew up she became aware of her two big, romping brothers, even then protective and kindly, but focused on things that were incomprehensible to her. There were shouts of laughter, sometimes of exasperation, over papers on which they wrote and painted, and involved allusions and private jokes which made

Jason, the eldest, screw up his face to show he under-stood everything. Then there were boisterous games that frightened her, and other games that were more like the rituals of a secret society, continuing day after day down by the pond, carving chalk castles and marshalling armies of hips and haws. Everything was resolved into images of war: the air became alive with scarcely contained aggression, ideas of defence, attack and mobilisation. Though repelled, she was also attracted by their latent masculinity, or perhaps simply by the fact that there were two of them, and they represented a family soli-darity so far unknown to her.

But it was a hermetic solidarity, proof against intru-sion, and she retired to her house in the bay tree. In the distance she heard their voices, not reaching her but running parallel, reassuring in the long summer morning. Everything was going as it should, and soon Nan would bring her a glass of milk and she might tiptoe past Howard sitting on the terrace, his feet planted flat on the gravel, buried in his newspaper. Aware of that strange, empty, bell-jar feeling at midday, she would go in to have her lunch separately, alone with Nan.

And then there was Jamie; to what could she liken Jamie's eyes? Neither sage nor cornflowers, but to some grey-blue stone perhaps of which she didn't know the name. They were large and round, wide apart, and showed only that he was enjoying himself, nothing deeper, but in that enjoyment there was a hint of intimacy, the offering, could she but grasp it, of a secret. His dreams, plain and obvious to him, remained essentially mysterious to Bettina. Rather than revealing things she longed to know, his apparent innocence – so false – seemed to conceal them, as furniture is shrouded when the owner is absent or as the clown whitens his face and reddens his lips to disguise the fact that, underneath, he too is a man.

There was certainly something clown-like about Jamie. It was not only that – a natural original – he often said or did things that provoked laughter but, like classic clowns and fools, he seemed to have been born free, unenslaved to the needs and motivations that most people struggle with. He wanted nothing for himself, not money, possessions or that insidious thing: power. If Bettina loved him more than anyone she knew, it was doubtless for this reason. He asked for so little – never anything she could not give him, and so she wanted to give everything. But still his eyes, sparkling, affectionate and amused as they were, never warmed up to a greater heat, never expressed anything more intense; only very occasionally she saw in them a mute misery like that of an animal. It seemed as though, his other qualities being so rare, he had been deprived at birth of the capacity to be completely human – and perhaps he adopted the costume of the clown to disguise it.

Although the kitchen was not her true territory, Maman's presence was felt there even when she was absent. The further away she was, the less they could forget her, and were all anxious to make up for it when she came back. It was as though an evening shadow lay across the path. They said: 'Oh, your mother wouldn't like it,' or 'Mrs Willoughby wants it done this way,' in low tones as though it were a law they must obey. They were in awe of her because of her stateliness, her calm superiority. She was mistress of the household, and they the servants.

How aloof she seemed, how monumental she looked, standing in the dark kitchen, her white hair drooping in two folds over her high forehead, puckered as usual into a frown of perplexity. There were people coming to lunch and they were to have a pheasant shot last week by Howard; but the main task was to prevent Lettice from making some awful pudding which she was in a fever to do, it being one of her specialities. She dreamed at night of brilliantly coloured jellies wobbling in glass bowls, and trembled as she suggested one for the occasion. Of course Mrs Willoughby wouldn't have it. She wanted something else, just a plain apple pie, because the boys liked it – and even then it must be cold, because that was what they preferred – and probably made the day before.

Standing beside Mrs Willoughby, Lettice barely came up to her shoulder. She trembled like a leaf in the breeze, whether with nervousness or irrepressible vitality no one could be sure. Unlike the proverbial cook she was as thin as a mannequin and dressed in clothes that might have been passed down to her, on the bottom rung of the social ladder, from some fashionable friend of Howard's. She was inordinately proud of her legs, sometimes likened to those of Mistinguett, and wore high heels, even though they were more tiring, because to her Mistinguett meant glamour. She had been a foundling, left on the doorstep of the old hospital in a basket, how long ago no one quite knew. She had no parents and no home but she was a Londoner all right, and somehow for that reason her hair was a shade or two blacker than it really should have been, while her nose ended in a red button, which she constantly rubbed. It may have been true that she spent her wages on whisky – no one knew for sure – but when all was said and done, she really was an excellent cook.

Mrs Willoughby's morning visit to the kitchen was something of an ordeal for Lettice because surrounding her mistress was a crowd of other things, things that Lettice thought of as ghosts. It was Mrs Willoughby's

Past. Wherever she went it followed her. It upset Lettice since what she liked was gaiety, fun – and when she worked for Howard in London, which she did most of the time, only coming down to the country for the summer holidays, he understood this. With him she felt both flattered and appreciated. He was happy to buy the best and left her free to indulge her fantasies of oceans of butter and cream, eggs and sugar. But Mrs Willoughby stood there with a family tradition of frugality behind her, looking so bored – and though she often said 'Yes', her smile somehow took the wind out of your sails. She meant to be kind, but it was easy to see she was living another life in another world, and couldn't really understand ordinary things. So Lettice giggled – which irritated Maman – and, almost volatilised in the heat of the kitchen, asked for an extra day off to go and see her friend Mabel, who worked for Mrs Willoughby's sister.

Of course Mrs Willoughby said 'Yes' to Lettice. She could go and see her friend whenever she liked. She could leave the evening meal ready prepared and Nan could lay the table for once. It would be no bother to anyone. But she said it with a tinge of cold impatience really addressed to herself, while a vision of her mother rose in her mind: of the servants in caps and aprons and their life in the cockroach-ridden Kensington basement. Things had, thank goodness, come quite a long way since those days,

17

a time that lay within her own memory though not in Lettice's. She thought of her mother's thin, careworn and noble profile, seeing it for the first time without glamour, without the shimmer that had surrounded it at a time when she, as the eldest of four, belonged to a sex that was – God knows why – destined to serve rather than to command. No wonder that her mother had so often been absent, eluding not only the cares of her own immense household but the myriad needs of cousins, nephews and nieces, all cravenly adoring. She could only manage to save her skin by giving instructions, by short, sharp words, saying 'Do' or 'Don't' – and by her unexplained disappearances.

But in looking at Lettice, who sometimes amused but more often exasperated her, Mrs Willoughby was unsure of having achieved anything. It irked her that Lettice so depended on her – why should the poor woman have to ask leave to see her friend? More disturbing still was the thought that she herself depended on the good services of another woman, someone who had fallen into her life by chance, someone for whom she could not feel a shred of human warmth or intimacy but whom she was forced, from fear of being left in the lurch, to treat with care.

And so Mrs Willoughby left the kitchen with relief, able to slough off, at least momentarily, her feelings of irritation, of swimming against the tide. Since it was in her house, the kitchen, she supposed, belonged to her – but it had little of her in it. True, it was filled with dishes and saucepans, frying-pans and ladles, some of which had been given to her on her wedding day and others that she had collected in different parts of the world. There were also little curtains she had put up in an effort to hide a dark corner, or a cupboard she had decorated. But it was the only room the servants had to themselves, the only space where they could spread themselves out. There were drawers filled with balls of string, old bitten pencils, sticky labels and blunt scissors, and other places where Lettice kept an odd handkerchief or two or a bottle of scent and a torn recipe book. There were corners into which Mrs Willoughby dared not look for fear of finding small mementoes of other lives lived alongside her own, but which had nothing to do with her and hardly responded to the same laws of nature. For her, the servants' lives represented a tangled mass of dark, confused feeling, which she could hardly bear to look at, fearful perhaps of seeing a reflection of a part of herself.

No doubt there were, deep down, feelings they shared, and in the recurrent crises of life Mrs Willoughby took on another dimension and became someone whose advice, if rather bald and lacking in warmth, could be relied upon for its honesty, even its practicality. It became clear to her at such moments that this was her true role in life, someone who, like the figurehead on a ship, ploughed her way through the high seas, both willing and able to take the brunt, buoyant like seasoned oak, conscious of a past that belonged to her alone, and that kept her afloat no matter what happened.

The life of her servants seemed to her raw and helplessly weak, and yet so powerfully real that it eluded her grasp, rushing through her and leaving her with a feeling of weakness that undermined her great strength. She went slowly along the corridor, her back a little bent with the strain of the experience but, before she reached the door of the studio, already smiling both at herself and them, seeing them now almost as children in her care.

It wasn't only works of art the grown-ups talked about. The favourite subject, as in any home, was people. But what happened to the people they talked about? Something strange – they were reduced to marionettes, puppets with jerky, disjointed movements on a different stage, where they scraped and bowed with staring eyes, belonging more to the past than the present. Bettina joined in the family discussions, feeling clever, encouraged to peel people's reality away from them, encouraged to be not cruel, but unkind. All she wanted was to shine, with no thought for others or the past or the future. And yet there were moments when she was shocked at the unkindness of the others and protested, only to be snubbed by the grown-ups. Something would make her quiver and screw herself up tightly as instantaneous as a sea-anemone or a limpet, and let the waves wash over her. All Bettina had was a feeling, no framework, no solid point of reference, no strength. She was ineffectual.

And then one afternoon Bettina, rushing from the garden into the house, fell on the brick floor and broke her front tooth. It was the first of those shocks that now, long afterwards, she could see had punctuated her life like miniature earthquakes, warnings of greater shocks to come. Not that the tooth was painful, or that she minded about the slight disfiguration which the old-fashioned, punctilious dentist said he would eventually put right. No, it was this peculiar feeling of shock, as though God had touched her on the shoulder and had said: 'Stop there!' It was nothing. And yet in some strange way it was a sign. So, smothered under Maman's anxiety, Bettina, aged eight, allowed herself to be a child again, and was coddled and made much of, thinking herself a special case because of her broken tooth.

Inside Bettina there was a hardness, a longing to cut things down to her own size so that she could dominate or master them. Why did she fail where others succeeded, why was she always outside the fence, running like a small white mare, but never drawing level? Until finally she refused to run and turned away: this has nothing to do with me, I will not compete. But she couldn't get away from herself, had always been taught to think of herself first, and now could do nothing else. And yet at the same time she had been taught it was wrong, so she pretended to be good. But being good was so dull and boring and, every now and again, suddenly shattered by reality.

The house was like a beehive, always glowing gently like a light seen under water. The sound of industry was low, insistent but private, addressed to no one. It was a perpetual act of self-purification, a pleasure, like a bird splashing in the pool on the lawn. Maman and Jamie refused all the ugly aspects of life, having only time for the dreams that veiled their eyes with private visions. They were unable to see cruder points of view, they shrank from violence and passion and had a strange ability to smother reality with ironic laughter. Their view prevailed and seemed all-powerful – delicious when you agreed but exasperating when you didn't.

Many people came to the house throughout the summers, the long series of summers that made up childhood. Their visits rang like a peal of bells leaping from one year to the next, expected, awaited with excitement.

Among them the White Knight with green hair and dark, golden eyes beneath bushy eyebrows. His whole being vibrated like the strings of a double bass, his voice trembling with a thousand different shades of meaning. His features were blunt, large, outsize, and he looked like Little Red Riding Hood's grandmother before, or, perhaps, after becoming the wolf – Bettina wasn't sure, only to be eaten by him might be a pleasure, she thought. Instead his long fingers did things he hoped would satisfy her, tying special knots that could not come undone, or that slipped loose at a touch, or sticking together pieces of cardboard or making a box without glue just by folding a piece of paper while, ecstatic, she was fascinated by his smiling concentration and stared at the cleft in his chin. It was the sense of power that went to her head, watching this vibrant man pretending to be her slave, the man who, above all others, everybody in the house wanted to monopolise.

Though amused, he was not heartless like some of the others. He never put you through your paces, you were not just a clockwork doll. His steel-rimmed spectacles circled his eyes, which were deep, reflective, seeing her as she was. He was trustworthy.

But he was also a figure of fun: arriving in an old car, throbbing with effort, tied together with string, stopping, starting, reversing in short bursts of energy – an uncontrollable monster needing to be placated with water and petrol. Always open to the elements (maybe its roof didn't shut), the car spread across the road like an armadillo, armoured but vulnerable and temperamental. Capacious, it held his canvases, his sketching easel, his suitcase as well as the tools he needed to tame it – they cluttered and filled the pockets on doors and rumbled under the back seat. When he wasn't in the car it was an extension of himself, as though his studio were on wheels. Gypsy at heart, his car was his caravan.

And yet he had built himself a house and had had a family – but this was long ago. Now all he had was Y who tried to reduce him by her laughter to proportions she could manage, which only resulted in more growth; like a tree pruned on one side he shot out on the other – unmanageable. Nothing could change him and he was incapable of seeing himself as others did.

The beauty of this life was that nothing ever happened. Each day stretched out indefinitely, leading inexorably to the next. Each day swelled like a luminous bubble, full of promise, till it reached a point where it almost burst, when the noises of the household changed key and everyone was conscious of having done their utmost. Rest and contentment had been earned, and the day, like a well-oiled Rolls-Royce, slowed down while the summer shadows, growing longer, swallowed it, wrapping up the household in a luxuriant living darkness, where such noises as there were, of a bird surprised or a cat on the prowl, echoed themselves away into the secrecy of the night.

The gifts the fairies had granted Bettina were unspectacular, but infinitely precious. Never scolded and untrammelled by unnecessary social conventions, she enjoyed an immense freedom, queering her way across the chessboard from one tall figure to another. Seemingly immovable and always tolerant – though infinitely detached – they looked on her, she now thought, as they might have looked at a tadpole in a bottle of formaldehyde: a form of life they had long ago forgotten about. The infinite patience of the grown-ups, their kindness and their jokes, fell on her from on high like petals from the cherry tree when the flowers were over.

Maman in the studio was different from Maman in the kitchen. In the studio she was queen, matriarch, a supreme if benign presence, whose permission had always to be asked. No one in the family would do anything without seeking it or, at the very least, forewarning her of their desires and intentions. She was invested with authority and felt that it was hers by right, although she was often bowed by the accompanying sense of responsibility. It took Bettina years to realise that Maman's image, in her eyes, was different from that in Jamie's. To him Maman was faultless or rather – as he didn't think in such terms – there was nothing in her he wished different or dreamed of changing. He needed her to be as she was: a bulwark, a reference and a support, splendid and compelling; this dependence had, like a stream winding its course down the valley, created its own bed. In the studio they fitted together perfectly and formed a whole, big enough for each other and largely oblivious of the world beyond.

They shared so much. Not only the excitement of what had, at the time, been the discovery of a new kind of painting, but the knowledge that, for each of them, art was the most important thing in life. And yet of course, over this statement hung a huge if invisible question mark. Since what, for Maman, could be more important than her children? What did she live for if not for Bettina and her brothers, so young, so vulnerable and dependent – deliciously dependent – on her?

But for Maman nothing was simple. The only complete, unalterable happiness was contained in the moment when she caressed the canvas with her brush, a gesture that visibly transferred her into another world, albeit one where she might be interrupted by Lettice, Nan or the housemaid – or the telephone (that recent installation that connected her with friends living beyond the orbit of the studio who seemed so distant). It was perhaps no wonder that she should react with a kind of freezing politeness towards this new invasion, putting off and discouraging any threat to her privacy. In fact, in this *vie de famille*, there was no such thing as privacy. The only solitude she knew was that which she could build round herself in the midst of everything that went on. Never alone, always in demand, whether as a critic of Jamie's work or as the comforter of Bettina in tears over some trifle, or questioned by the old man who worked in the garden as to what he should plant or sow in the vegetable patch, she never had even half an hour of pure concentration, pure communion with pinks and yellows.

And yet, Bettina felt in later years, trying to elucidate the mystery of Maman's life, it was not only this that implanted such a deep furrow between her eyes and made her stoop as though she carried the world on her shoulders. She was anxious, permanently anxious, as though catastrophe might strike her down at any moment. Being queen of all she surveyed was not enough to calm this anxiety – she needed more, always more of this unknown or at least unnamed quantity – an intense desire that had had an effect on Bettina as well, submerging her and drawing her in like a wave only to envelop her again to the point of suffocation. There was something about this desire of Maman's, which appeared to everyone else as not only natural but beautiful, that was, for Bettina, insufferable. It pretended to be generous and tender but underneath it lay, hidden from all but her, a hunger that was unappeasable. It was a bottomless pit of longing that scared her stiff and left her with a feeling of total inadequacy.

This was why Jamie's presence was essential to perfect happiness. His buoyancy and naturalness protected her a little from Maman's hunger, from the terrifying desire she seemed to have of reabsorbing Bettina into some dark, underground cavern and never letting go.

As the youngest of the family Bettina was the most vulnerable. Had she been older she might have been able to distance herself, or were she nearer to her brothers in age she might have belonged more to them and not been so on her own. Yet she was not only the youngest but also the only girl, and therefore something special. Realising this, she revelled in the attention – it fed her ever-hungry ego. She became a small monster in her own right, not only demanding but taking all she could get, as though secretly entitled to all the diamonds on earth. Becoming imperious, she was just laughed at, never reproached or scolded, nor did she ever succeed in upsetting the complacency of those who surrounded her. They remained unutterably calm: pipe smoking, like Howard, smiling, like Maman, or gently joking and elusive, like Jamie; only once could she remember, as the complexities of life began to dawn on her, guiltily comparing Maman with the mother of a friend of hers. 'Maman is cold,' she said. 'I envy you yours.' It was sacrilege to say such a thing, to speak of Maman as though there were a possibility of changing her for another, like a queen on the chessboard. But she quite often wished she could – not realising at that young age that her mother was human and fallible, subject to the same emotions as everyone else.

For Jamie, Maman was supreme, her judgement incontrovertible. Through her he enjoyed a family life he wouldn't have had otherwise, a stability and calm without boredom that, he felt, she alone could provide. He was aware of what she gave him; though he was not grateful, since gratitude seemed to him too moral an attitude and had little to do with his real feelings. He trusted her utterly, and took what she offered in all innocence, knowing that, as he needed her, she also needed him.

But, Bettina eventually realised, Maman and Jamie needed each other in very different ways: her need was hungry and possessive, his instinctive and undemanding. Had Maman refused to see him any more Jamie would not have died of it. Wounded perhaps, uncomprehending, but always ready to accept another's decision without

29

question, he would have gone his own way complete and self-sufficient, depending more on his art than on people for his spiritual sustenance. At the same time he was vulnerable: his feelings lay on the surface, apparent to all; limpid as a child's they also seemed as shallow, although what they lacked in depth they made up for in purity. Anyone could have taken advantage of him – and of course they often did; he had crowds of dim hangers-on who exploited his innocence and devoured his time and sometimes too his none too abundant money. They were often charming and frequently, though not always, of inferior social status. None of them had succeeded in life, and all of them felt they owed Jamie something indefinable but extraordinarily precious. Like King James, who, at the touch of his hand could cure people of the scrofula, Jamie, who had never tried to cure anyone of anything, gave out some quality which, like a natural spring of pure water, had a beneficial effect. Those who had tasted it once always came back for more. He seldom refused them unless Maman, a trifle exasperated, pointed out what a waste of time they were. Eventually he took to seeing these friends mostly in London, a situation that Maman accepted with a philosophic smile. This smile seemed full of tenderness and love to Jamie; but for Bettina it held an element of superiority, even arrogance. She couldn't quite define it but it betrayed a feeling she resented. The smile, like that of the *Mona Lisa*, was not one of collusion, but of permission granted, yet only through suffering and only in the strong, almost sepulchral light of Maman's own needs and desires. Nothing she did was ever quite straightforward and always partly veiled in reticence so that, although one of the most generous of women, there was always something she withheld, something she could not relinquish and instead she offered her smile. Jamie had an extraordinary ability to disregard anything ambiguous and so the smile had no effect on him. He took things at face value or touched them with a magic wand and turned them into a joke. So Maman was teased for her reservations, her odd, sudden refusals to like something such as, for example, Brighton. For Bettina, and also probably for Jamie, Brighton was sparkling, fresh and delicate, bathed in the white light of the south and full of old shops selling mementoes of past times, enticing the visitor to linger in narrow, dusty streets which, leading downhill, finally brought them face to face with the sea. But nothing could induce Maman to go there. She had suffered too much in the past, she said, from a family of cousins who lived in Hove.

Bettina could not understand this. The pleasure of the moment seemed to her infinitely more important than those queer things called memories, of which she, the youngest, had so few compared to anyone else. For Maman, however, Brighton and Hove had been excised as though cut out of the map with a pair of sharp scissors. The present had no power to dissolve that shadowy area, about which she would – alas – say very little, but which in Bettina's mind was inhabited by a crowd of ghosts, thin young women clad in black with ambiguous smiles like Maman's, bending over their young cousin with hypocritical intent. In later years she realised that she had probably not been so wrong about this, that they had in some way poisoned Maman's mind and that revulsion had extended to Brighton. How she wished Maman had been more explicit, more communicative. It was only now, at the age of seventy and long after Maman's death, that, in searching through the past, Bettina had found whole areas of darkness about which Maman had never spoken. As a child she had not been interested enough, she supposed, to provoke such confessions and Maman too had allowed her inhibitions to overcome her and, rationalising, had thought she wouldn't worry her daughter with memories that, after all, no longer mattered.

At the age of nine, Bettina felt, for no particular reason she could give, that she had made an immense leap forward – as in the game of Grandmother's Steps, she felt she had made a move in the dark when no one was looking. She had, she thought, become more capable, more independent, more self-sufficient – all things ostensibly encouraged by Maman who already foresaw, and apparently longed for, a future when Bettina would be a princess, courted by all the most interesting young men, free to bestow her favours where she wished.

In the evenings Maman would read the classics aloud, her beautiful cool, low voice running around the words, setting them for ever in a marble mould. Often the 'others', the grown-ups, would come and listen too, and afterwards discuss the character and behaviour of the heroes and heroines, who were then dissected and pinned like iridescent butterflies to the board, fixed into enthralling if frozen attitudes. Emma, Jane, Dorothea, Elizabeth and Lucy were talked of as if they had been personal friends, now dead of course, but still alive in the minds of those present, those who had known them in other times, well before Bettina's day, but were now handing them over to her, enjoying the impression they made on her. Thus encouraged, she had no difficulty in entering the characters' situations, investing herself in their lives, either the self-consciously good behaviour, the porcelain glow of Jane Austen or the wild, storm-ridden rigours of *Jane Eyre*. Encouraged to identify, she did so completely, immersing herself in a past that seemed to belong to everyone, particularly of course to Maman, through whose being Bettina could stretch back to that shadowy Victorian age of inhibited passionate longings where women struggled for freedom but never got it.

It was perhaps odd that the men – Darcy, Rochester, Heathcliff and the others – were not so real to her. And yet, though she could not see them sitting down to breakfast or going for a walk with her, they had a mysterious power to attract, possessed, apparently, by no one she actually knew. By living in books, however, she could bask in the complete, mesmeric attention of Darcy or Rochester and the flattery of being treated as a woman, mature yet vulnerable, whom they wished to protect and possess.

In some strange, subliminal way Bettina was beginning to be aware of what sexual possession meant. She took it for granted that man was attracted by woman and vice versa. It was such an evident fact of life: people lived in pairs – and they usually had children. The world was made that way and it seemed on the whole rather boring. It had nothing to do with Mr Rochester or Mr Darcy. In her own everyday life sex shone by its absence. The beds, most of them uncomfortable, were also single. No one shared one with anyone else. Neither Howard nor Jamie gave Maman more than a peck on the cheek when they returned from an absence. No one unnecessarily touched anyone else. No one exuded that desirable and mysterious quality that belonged only, it seemed, to Mr Darcy or Mr Rochester. There was safety in this probably, but no thrill and no warmth. She lived in a paradise from which the serpent had long ago departed.

And paradise, although glowing and golden, was a lonely place. Bettina was hardly aware of it, since in many ways she enjoyed her solitude, but it reduced her to living alone with her dreams and produced in her the faraway look of someone who is often not at home, who cannot be found where you expect her to be even when you knock at the door. It became evident that paradise, though as hallucinatory, as attractive as ever, was not where she wanted to be. The serpent had, very possibly, bitten her in the night – but the effect had been paralytic. Bettina now hid all her strongest and most intimate feelings, afraid that even Maman would find a way of scorching her with a cold flame of derision. Nothing made Bettina feel more inadequate or exposed, as though she suddenly found herself stranded on a ledge of rock high above the sea, unable to take the plunge and swim with the others. Instead she cowered, and was ashamed. Maman, though well-meaning was not to be trusted. Bettina hid everything from her, remembering how on one occasion, when her brother Jason had said something wounding to her, she had retired to her bedroom at the top of the house to weep bitter tears alone but, on hearing Maman's rather heavy footstep on the stairs, had quickly dried them with the back of her hand and had started brushing her hair, which hung like a curtain between them. Maman, disappointed, had been at a loss and unable to explain the reason for her irruption into Bettina's room. This non-event, this silly incident, had been one of the first to sour their relationship.

In later years she occasionally wondered how different her life might have been had she had a sister. She dreamed of intimacies and collusions as well as disagreement, even bitterness and fierce competition. But she might have emerged tougher and closer to other human beings, with a feeling she was one among many instead of someone who was always, for indefinable reasons, different and apart.

Her family itself was different. Within its polished, white circle it radiated confidence, just as the walls of the house radiated colours. And the colours, so different from those you might have found on the walls of any other house, not only protected but isolated them. This circle, drawn by Maman and Jamie, quivered with life. Like an electric fence, it kept people both in and out.

No one could stay inside all the time, and Bettina noticed that even Maman, when she found herself elsewhere, was ill at ease. She could not adapt, like Jamie, but instead, always feeling that the fault lay with her, had the unfortunate effect of inhibiting the other person. Incapable of being light and easy-going, devastatingly innocent of all the common props that might have helped her (such as an interest in political or social events), she often seemed bare as a tree in winter. Like a tree she stood tall and made a tremendous impression, often rather a desolate one, Bettina felt, and quite unlike that of other mothers who, though less impressive, were more approachable.

Outside the brittle circle of family life Bettina knew next to nothing. Only the weekly dancing class at a house in Hampstead, or the extraordinary yearly plunge into the remote Norfolk village where Nan's sister lived – this was an experience as different from home as chalk from cheese. But these did not help to illuminate Bettina's problem. Nan's sister Helen was a farmer's wife: she dealt with gallons of milk and pints of cream and made butter in a churn. She fed the dogs and the sow and served the men with their dinner, for which she would make a thick, solid Yorkshire pudding. At night, at an hour when at home Maman would be sitting down under the lamp to answer her letters, Helen and her husband Jack would tramp upstairs to bed, saying they were too tired to do more – and Bettina, her small limbs scratched by briars and glowing with fatigue after a long day on the farm, would by then be fast asleep, comforted in her dreams by the memory of Helen's rough and ready kindness and the knowledge that Jack would tease her mercilessly in the morning before he set off to work.

There was no mystery here. The difference between this and her home life was open and straightforward, which was, probably, the reason Bettina loved it. Helen and Jack were as ordinary as a basket of potatoes or a couple of apples hanging on a tree. With them she knew where and who she was, for the time being at least, whereas, when she got home again – a home she had at times longed for during the months away – she was subject to the queer, almost physical effect of metamorphosing into a different little girl. She had only to see Maman waiting for her in the hall, ready to hug her so closely for one brief second, and then to say something to Nan over her head which at once reduced Nan from being Maman's substitute – with whom Bettina was, in many ways, more intimate than she was with Maman – to being plain and slightly anxious Nan, who worked on the other side of the squeaking doors. In that one, impossible second, she had slipped back into being Bettina, the spoiled and youngest of the family, living in an uncertain state of knowing and not knowing. She could no longer happily forget herself, fraternising with the animals on the farm or the kind and almost equally oblivious haymakers in the field, but was coaxed, prodded and provoked by the all too articulate members of her family into what she could now see was the beginning, the half-unconscious and painful intimations of self-awareness.

This was one of the differences, shared by all of them and – more important than she could possibly have realised – setting them all ineluctably apart as though someone in the past had built a wall of glass between them and the world through which they could see, but not feel or touch. For her Helen and Jack were real. The sound of their voices vibrated with warmth and some other quality less easy to define, something that rang with a density and authority that rose from an unknown depth, as though you had dropped a stone into a well. But she was the only one of the family who knew them well. For the others Jack and Helen were merely a fact, a happy one perhaps, which removed Bettina from their sight for a time, but never became palpable, never, as they were to her, warm and living. When her brother Jason asked her where she had been and what she had been doing, words would not form in her mouth. She could only look dreamy and hang her head, her smile disappearing almost before he could catch it, even though she stood caught between his stalwart knees, reassured by his geniality, the warmth of his sudden, all too brief interest. Almost at once however, in a single night, Jack and Helen became unreal. They faded and became memories, floating downstream, every day further away and less visible.

Her family itself was different. This was a fact Bettina had always known and as she grew up she automatically became one of them, the small band of those who were 'different'. Now she had to put it in inverted commas as she began to realise she hardly knew what it really meant. It was a reality she grew up with – sometimes a matter of pride and, as she got older, something that became an almost palpable barrier which she longed to batter down.

But battering down was out of the question. This was too primitive a reaction and would have made no sense. How could you batter a stalwart tweed-coated man like Howard, who sat in the garden and smoked a pipe with such ineffable enjoyment, or how entertain the faintest thought of violence towards Maman whose equally in-effable sweetness had a way of dissolving anything that might resemble a rebellion, particularly one as small and fragile as Bettina's.

Within its polished, brittle world the family quivered with energy and confidence, above all with a laughter that echoed round and round the house, transforming it into a place that was unique and like no other place on earth. Bettina thought of it as though it floated in the sky, recalling the Holy City as painted by Bellini and other old masters. These paintings had always puzzled her, since how and why should a whole city, small as it evidently was, float unattached in the air? Would she find the same brightly coloured walls and demonic shrieks of laughter? Had she painted the city herself she might, she thought, have put a few demons issuing energetically from the windows, waving red flags and calling out to the indifferent world. In the paintings the people on the ground must know the city is there, but they pay it no attention. Yet Bettina knew that, were she in one of these pictures, she would want to know more about the magic city. Her eyes would have been turned upwards, and perhaps one of the demons would have made her a secret sign. She would, in fact, have been someone special, singled out for a different future.

Was it because of a certain unreality that the family could not afford to live there all the time – afford, that is to say, the luxury of its being too good to be true? The great point of being there was, Maman said, the quality of the light, the pool of light in which the house always lay. It was evidently something extremely special, so much so that everyone silently nodded in a kind of suspended agreement. For Bettina it was a remark that stayed high in the air, remote and unreal. One that she might understand and even make use of later, but, for the present, what significance did it have beside the fact that there she could run as fast as possible down the white strip of hard, flinty road with the sun on her back, as far as she liked to go, with the sound of cows and plovers in her ears and the smell of manure in her nostrils?

The necessity of leaving the house and going to London was, however, built into their lives. It was inevitable, like the flow of the tide or the migration of swallows, and was a habit followed by most, if not all of their friends. They needed the real city, not the visionary one – the soot-black forest of London, flaming secretly at night and umber-coloured by day. Seen thus, one could suddenly understand what Maman meant by the quality of the light. If you wanted to draw a picture of London you would have to do it in charcoal, smudging it darkly on a piece of grainy paper, and the only animal you could include would be the basement cat, rubbing its hungry back against the dustbin, or the patient carthorse, its hooves clopping over the asphalt.

There was no difference so potent, or so weird, as that made by people. London was so full of people you could not possibly count them, yet those who emerged from the crowd and became recognisable individuals left a mark in the air – sometimes even a mark on you. You never knew, from day to day, who you might meet; in the country you only met those who, as part of the family, were meant to be there. The game you played there, in spite of the occasional surprise, was one you knew by heart and therefore deliciously soothing. Its rhythms were repetitive and slow, like an adagio by some ageless, untroubled composer, who simply wrote down his notes without *arrière-pensée*. The days started with the lowing of cows, and ended with the hoot of the owl and the sensation of the immense, dark spaces surrounding you as you lay in your primitive iron bed.

But in London, while there was a certain excitement, there was also *angoisse*. The spaces were no longer made of airy velvet, but were shot through with moving lights and shadows and the roar, distant but menacing, of the London traffic, dimly felt by Bettina as the roar of all those who were a part of this monstrous thing called London.

In the morning the prevailing smell would be one of soot, and the light, filtered through the plane trees, almost non-existent. Porridge, considered wholesome, would seem tasteless, and milk, far from being creamy white, would be thin and blue. Warmth came from a gas fire that could be turned on and off, and also from the voices in the basement kitchen, where everyone always seemed happier than those who lived upstairs. Bettina would hear them in her brown nursery solitude, waiting for Nan to bring up the pot of tea without which, it seemed, life for her here lost much of its meaning. The pressures in

London required something like six or seven strong cups of tea a day, and it was only after Nan had swallowed down her first of the day, thickened and strengthened with milk and sugar, that she would say in her Norfolk accent, her red cheeks polished like apples, that it was time to go. There were habits in London just as in the country, of course, but they seemed of a different nature, no longer the sound of an adagio, but dictated by the incessant demands of people who had decided that this queer, disjointed tempo was the way to live.

Bettina was not without friends of her own – they were either the children of Maman's friends, or those she made at school. One of these, a little girl called Rose, often came to stay and, although she was not obviously attractive in any way, was accepted by the family with a sigh of relief, since now Bettina would no longer be liable to erupt at any moment into the superior world of the grown-ups, claiming the attention with phenomenal, if transparent, egotism.

Bettina envied Rose her mother – a fragile little woman who stood on the doorstep of a large, sombre house in a London square, saying goodbye to Rose as Bettina carried her off. She hardly needed to know more about her, since she was able to deduce, from seeing the tender, familiar way they embraced, that their relationship was intimate and that, even though Dr Trelawney might be dead – a fact that conferred some distinction on Rose – the resulting sadness was not all-devouring.

Travelling alone on the train, Rose would arrive at their house in the country, met of course by Jamie or Jason at the station and driven bumpily over the intervening miles, to be welcomed by Maman as though she were a leaf drifted off a tree, arrested in her faltering flight just before being lost for ever. For Rose, Maman was an assurance of feminine solidarity, and although her own behaviour expressed nothing if not trust, she did seem out of place, the two families being so different.

But Bettina and Rose, Rose and Bettina appeared to amalgamate. They became one, and did everything together, behaving, as Bettina now saw it sixty years later, exactly as Maman and all the grown-ups expected them to. In the long, hot month of August, they spent a lot of time either deep in the endless, mindless conversation of little girls, or in another life, constructed by themselves as a kind of answer, like a reflection in the pond, to the duller, more rigid and less romantic existence of the grown-ups.

When the toll of the dinner bell sounded at midday, echoing over the tufts of thick grass from where the larks rose in the morning, the two children knew it was time to submit to authority and custom. Like Alice, they willingly ate that part of the mushroom that reduced them to their normal size, and took their places at the round family table in the dining room which always seemed capable of accommodating any number of visitors. Everyone was there, Jamie, Howard, her brothers Jason and Giles – sometimes also a friend or two from London.

Then the conversation began, breathed on each day, like the carefully tended embers, carried from one camping site to another by Red Indians. The eternal smile on Maman's face was subtle, changing and responsive; just as she never laughed outright, she never straightforwardly condemned. Her choices were narrow, foreseeable and often negative. Bettina took it for granted she would never want to go for a walk, and never join in a game. She would nearly always prefer staying at home, spending her time, if possible, standing brush in hand in front of her easel absorbed by an intense communion with a vase of red-hot pokers, those strangely phallic flowers that grew almost wild in the garden.

Sometimes Bettina hated the truth, not only because it said something she did not want to hear, but because, facing it head-on, she felt damned. Why was it that, in spite of the imagination, the intelligence she knew she possessed, she had never written or painted a master-piece? It was not from a lack of a sense of shape or an idea, or the ability to transcend, to rise and float over the earth like a Zeppelin. She paused, remembering the airship she had seen as a child, hanging low over the Downs – how beautiful it had been, in its silence. That might have been me, she thought, but the truth is that I never rose to that height, in spite of all possible encouragement. It was not lack of goodwill on the part of others, but the fact that, perhaps aping poor misguided Maman, who thought that for me to say 'No' would be a sign of poverty and defeat for herself, I never learned to pronounce the 'No' that inevitably implies a 'Yes' and would have, as I think now, opened the door to reality. It's not that I would have forsaken the world that I loved and lived in, but I would have had in my grasp a yardstick. I would have understood my relationship to that world, and not been so afraid of it.

As she suddenly realised, learning how to say 'No' involved saying 'Yes'. There might, of course, be long periods of time in which you floated, as on a raft, between two choices, knowing that the moment in which to say 'Yes' had not yet arrived. But it was there somewhere, it was implicit. The problem lay in recognising which 'Yes' it should be. Sometimes this involved a lot of time, a lot of courage, studying the reflection in the water. Bettina was afraid she had often lost her nerve and allowed her raft to dock too soon. She had not learned to listen to the oracle, to the only voice capable of telling her what to do. She had listened instead to the voices of reason and analysis which had drowned that faint but welcome echo that was only to be heard if you put your ear to the shell and listened in stillness and self-forgetfulness.

There is nothing wrong, is there, in wanting to be loved? But there is something frightening in a longing as strong as Maman's, and Jamie could only save himself from being devoured by an outright refusal. He could not help Maman understand where she had gone wrong and so she had to suffer in silence. Even Jason could not help her since they were too close: she had already poisoned him with her excessive love. And Howard had long ago shown himself to be too lazy, too much of an egotist to get involved.

But it was Maman who fertilised a certain atmosphere that was in itself encouraging. Without her these marvels would not have existed, even Jamie's strokes of genius would have fallen to the ground unnoticed. And of course, as Bettina saw with almost unbounded admiration, Maman contributed her own voice, so different from Jamie's, so deep, strong and individual, even though she never stopped saying how much she owed him. It was a partnership. And how could you have a partnership where one partner did not lean, at least a little, on the other? Like Philemon and Baucis they were entwined in mutual support. There was nothing wrong with this, felt Bettina, but what was so disturbing was what went on beneath the surface, among the hungry and twisted roots.

Maman was a monument, and as such was to be revered. There was something primordial, primitive and ruthless in her beneath the surface; while above it she was not only wise, tolerant and benign, but full of humour. This complexity, these contradictions – both her strengths and her weaknesses – gave her an immense depth and richness despite the fact that she allowed her weak points to drag her down into agonies of guilt. It was this sense of guilt that led her, a giantess, to try to hide herself behind a flimsy structure of protest that any of us could have discredited or knocked down with a single blow. But none of us had the necessary imagination or love to do so.

Bettina was perhaps over-sensitive to Maman's monolithic quality. She wanted to emulate it, to be like her, and, because she never could be, she was also perhaps jealous, envious of her far-reaching, effortless authority, of her power over other people. She felt Maman as a mould, a pattern, something to be understood as a warning, something to be avoided – in fact very much not to be. And for Bettina, as for Maman, there was no one for her to talk to, no one to give advice or help except, finally, Jason.

*   *   *

It was September: the point at which the holidays ended and a new life would begin. Bettina and Maman both found themselves together in the drawing room at that particular moment. Afterwards she did not remember Maman having called for her, but there they were and there too a certain atmosphere had arisen like a genie from a bottle. She found herself in Maman's arms where she felt much too big. She was no longer a little girl after all, listening to the sad but caressing voice telling her things she did not want to know. Her mind wandered and then returned, sucked into a vortex – she suddenly understood: Jamie was her father and not Howard.

Something had sprouted like a button mushroom, round, satisfactory and at the same time not new – she had known it was there as she might know something was under the hay in the field. It was a conjunction, two beings drawn together, belonging to each other, fitting together. Nevertheless Maman's voice was unreal, too sweet, too amused. What was her purpose? Maman clasped her knees with her long, knobbed fingers, and looked down, her heavy lids dropping like shutters over her eyes. 'It makes no difference really – you love Jamie just the same, though perhaps it will be better not to mention it to Howard. He likes to think of you as his.' The idea flashed through Bettina's mind that she loved Jamie – how surprising – but again confusion swallowed her. How could it make no difference? It made all the difference in the world! But Maman did not want her to talk about it. That was evident. And yet now she knew who her father was. Still she was to be thought of as someone else's daughter. There was still a mystery. It bound her as she stared beyond the French windows at the apple tree, the grass and the flint walls. She felt encircled, a hopeless beating of wings on glass. The luxury of being Jamie's daughter could be enjoyed without confronting him – the knowledge itself was enough. She would be a princess in disguise, yet, as she eventually realised, Jamie was an unsatisfactory father – perhaps he had never really wanted to be one. His real children were his paintings. And Howard, although he would have liked to be her father, was, for all sorts of reasons, prevented. And so Bettina grew up without the support she needed.

And then there was the world of the river. Day after day, Bettina and the boys would sneak off, taking their tea in a basket. It was too far to walk – they had to drive in Jason's old, shambly Morris. The open hood exposed them to the hot, dusty summer air, which swept, abrasive, past their faces. Bathing suits were crammed into a bag with some towels, and the rubber dinghy, recalling a reptile in the zoo, lay in black folds in the boot. Bettina sometimes took a book to read in the grass after tea was over, but though she had good intentions, she would seldom pick it up. It was too exciting, after eating great slices of fruit cake, to paddle in the dinghy between the islands of waterlilies – slung too low between the banks of rushes and loosestrife for her to be able to see the fields on either side. The water was sluggish and slow, darkly reflecting the cloud-flecked sky, its flow obstructed by the waterlily leaves and shadowy weeds lying beneath the surface.

From the boat, lying down, all she could see was the sky, all she could hear were the larks trilling, high above her like kites on a string. She was suspended in time and space, and so could invent what she pleased. Only the clouds raced ahead, as though to some enormously important world conference. But though they piled themselves imposingly on the periphery of Bettina's view, the sun, sinking lower already, bathed them in apricot and rose, and rendered them inoffensive. Bettina was an Indian in South America, with thousands and thousands of miles to go before she reached the sea. Perhaps there was a boa constrictor round the next corner or, more likely, a village of enemy Indians, who must be placated with the gold and turquoises she had brought from the Andes. But when she had rounded the corner, she saw a fence sloping down the bank into the water, and a red and white cow, dipping its soft, hairy lips nose-deep into the pool.

Even at fifteen, she sometimes played games of this

kind, until shaken out of them by the more robust demands of her brother. Jason sometimes rigged a sail, and then they would tack across the lower reaches of the river, where it was greyer and wider and slashed with small wavelets which lapped noisily against the elephantine rubber prow. Bettina would duck to avoid the tiny boom, and duck again, getting colder and wetter each time. But it was beneath her to admit her misery. She must at all costs be as good as he, this great brute of a fellow who weighed down the boat behind her. Jason would shout in excitement, 'Bettina, down with your head, down, girl.' And she would get more and more tired, but at the same time exalted, stung with sea air, her lungs swelling with the wild breezes blowing off the coast. And finally, there was the tide turning, coming up the river, a thrilling and inexorable counter-current, something utterly real from the great ocean, that even Jason could do nothing to control. It made their crooked progress slower and less certain. But finally the banks of the river widened, became sandy and barren. Seagulls swooped and screamed in aggressive frenzy, and she and Jason saw the chalk cliffs standing over the green sea, as they had stood since the beginning of England.

But at seventeen she had changed. Now when she stepped out of the car she was self-conscious. Her skirt was longer, and she tripped sedately behind a bush to undress, carrying a large wrap to hide her nudity. And then, just when a weekend visitor happened to look her way, things sometimes slipped revealing a shining thigh, or a small breast under a raised arm. Knowing the weakness of her defences, Bettina felt shy as she walked towards the boat, clothed only in last year's swimsuit, divided into three areas of red, white and blue. When the handsome, mature Edward gave her his arm, she leaned on it a little too long, overcome by a fantasy of swooning into his arms and being revived with brandy. And then she heard him saying that the other girl in the party, Jane, had been so graceful, so light of foot – in comparison with herself, she presumed. A pang of rage and shame shot through her, never to be forgotten, even now as a smiling old woman of seventy.

At seventeen, Bettina felt it was indescribably wonderful to have a brother ten years older than her. Jason was so full of life, so authoritative and yet a little unpredictable, plunging about as though he did not quite know where his strength lay. Whatever he did was bound to overwhelm her, to drown her in a great swirl of jubilation or anger. She never knew exactly where she stood, and felt that, whatever she achieved, she would never catch up. He knew so much more than she did, and the thought never came to her to distrust him. Sometimes, when Jason crushed Bettina with rough impatience, and she responded in fiery revolt and protest, he reduced her spirit of independence to impotence in a second; and then once more she would cling to him and hang around his neck, wheedling and pleading for what she wanted. Never, Bettina realised, did she tell the truth and say she wanted love and affection – and for some reason it was impossible to be natural and straightforward – but Jason would smile and good-naturedly accept her shortcomings. Then sometimes he would appease her hunger and sit with her, encircled by her small arms, his eyes narrowed in a smile, his own arms, strong and brown, holding her close. She was never satisfied and never had enough. Was she not growing up, and would she always be reduced to subterfuge to get what she wanted?

And yet she was not being fair: Jason was aware of her as she really was, more than anyone. There were times, in the garden under the moon, when he walked and talked with her, seeing she was so hypersensitive and *difficile*, and made her talk about herself – about what she felt, about what she hoped for. It was then that she tried to express her abstract consuming fear – she could not explain it, but she described to him how it oppressed her. Even poor Jason was puzzled rather than convinced, though she knew he had genuinely tried to understand her.

They talked too about Milton, Shakespeare and Shelley, and then Jason would betray a tenderness that showed itself in his voice, like a sudden gush of wine into a glass, and he would listen to her half-digested ideas and preferences, suggesting new authors for her to read. He gave her his first collection of poems, inscribed and dedicated to her and Maman, making her feel like a sixteenth-century countess, painted very small on a piece of jewellery.

Her trouble was that everything made her feel over-special and over-cared-for. Of course it was also her own fault since she could keep up nothing for long and would accept too easily the superficial reflection of herself she saw in other people's faces and the wild hopes of success she was encouraged to entertain: Bettina the Great, the Dazzling, the Marvellous. Still, when she reflected, she had to admit that at best she was a mere streak of summer lightning, not ever as bright as she ought to have been.

And then next to her there was always Jason, passionately serious about social questions, politics, elections – things that seemed unreal to her. One day he came and asked her to canvass for him in their local town. She went from door to door along the backsides of little, grey houses inhabited by women with permed hair and scant aprons, whose expressions, defensive and suspicious when they saw how young she was, took refuge in an attempt at frigid politeness. Soon she was tired out, too numbed by new impressions to understand what it was all about.

She vowed never to do it again. Perhaps it was Jason's passion – the violence only just contained, the strength of his expressions, his swearing and rumbustiousness – that so often swept away his delicious good humour. His voice would rise, anguished and frustrated, provoked in an argument with Howard. Bettina could not understand what they were talking about, only the strength of the emotion that had them in tow, and which shocked and horrified her. She wanted only to escape into Maman's calm atmosphere, which she knew nothing could disturb.

There were of course times when the siblings quarrelled, even in Maman's presence. Jason, so much older, had always had his own way, and rode roughshod over everyone – it was only Maman who could soothe him into a semblance of contrition. Her deep, cool voice poured on his heated temperament the oil he needed; but Bettina, as the only girl, was also cherished and spoiled. There were ugly quarrels over ridiculous subjects, such as what to play on the gramophone or which poem she should read; but Bettina seemed incapable of thinking things out – as a fighter she was useless. Her emotions flickered like small flames, and then went out.

He was not a brother to go dancing with; nor someone who could initiate her into social rites. One could see that he was almost as afraid of such things as she was herself, only in a different way – despising them and not wanting, as she did, to succeed. Yet occasionally to please her, when she had wheedled and kissed him enough (or too much), he would hold out his arms of a giant, seize her round the waist and, putting on a Cheshire Cat grimace, would waltz her clumsily round the room. He had no idea of rhythm or time, could not sing a melody, nor could he control his immense feet; but he would give a performance of sinuous femininity, of a geisha with a fan, or a Chinese lady mincing on pattens. Half exasperated by his clumsiness and half dissolved in laughter, Bettina trod on his toes, eluded his grasp, danced by herself and then returned to him. But he was no Prince Charming, there was nothing svelte or elegant about him. He was at ease in the countryside, striding in deep grass, in mud, over ploughland and up the hills, a dog at his heels, the wind in his hair, and in his pocket a little red Shakespeare.

And yet he loved parties, he loved pretty – or even not so pretty – girls. Some deep warmth in him, some capacity to love and appreciate, charmed them. He listened, deeply interested, and submerged himself in what the girls said, in what they were and what they wanted to be, made them feel valued, even trusted. His awkwardness, intensity and smiling acquiescence touched women. They told him secrets they would not have given away to another man, in the same way Bettina trusted him with hers. He loved women for what they were, not wanting to change them, just as he venerated Maman. Bettina watched them together, how, like a knight returned from battle, he would kneel on one knee, his face lit with unconscious adoration. Did Bettina feel a trifle excluded? Yes, she had to admit she did, knowing she could never feel like that herself, not at least for Maman – but perhaps for Jason.

Growing up was so strange. From feeling like a worm trodden underfoot, in the space of an instant Bettina became a princess, supple as a sapling, no thoughts in her head but with a feeling of marvellous strength and elasticity. She knew that she changed people simply by looking at them and knew also that, if she wished, they would do as she wanted. Like a tiger, or an angel, she found she could do anything.

At the age of nineteen Bettina felt she was grown up. She had a lover, called Bartle, wise and mature – a great deal older than she was. She loved him, though not as she would love someone she intended to spend the rest of her life with. She had known him for a long time. He was like an oak tree, reassuring and protective. She felt she could tread safely; and she loved being loved. Here was the knight errant kneeling on one knee again, but this time to her rather than to Maman. Now the smiles, the tenderness, the care and admiration were for her, and like a princess she accepted them.

Bettina moved away from home and lived with a crowd of young people. Here something happened to her, something that grew like lightning, took her breath away and left her almost fainting with delight and joy. The son of the owner of the new house, Daniel, was tender, caring and admiring – an admiration that, Bettina felt, was for her alone and not one that had first to be approved of by Maman. She responded to it in all its spontaneity and freshness, seeing herself for the first time as a young woman with a right to an existence of her own. Glowing with a secret pride, she was simply content – to help with the washing-up, to ensure that everyone had enough to eat, in a house that was now full of young people, who had come to act *Gammer Gurton's Needle* in their village hall.

Daniel was also older than she was, and gave her credit for what she might become, for those parts of her that still lay dormant. Could she only try with him, she might succeed in being what she wanted to be, however vague and unformed that notion was. So she let herself go, and allowed herself to float mindlessly in his wake. Even when he was not there she was buoyed up by the knowledge of his affection. She was neither cast down nor anxious, even when she saw him with another girl, Emma, who was far more sophisticated than she was, and who could hold her own in conversation with the older visitors who appeared in the house from time to time. Fine-featured and intelligent, well-read and kind too, she made Bettina feel like a child all over again. But it was rumoured that Emma's affair with Daniel was a thing of the past. And when Daniel returned, he made sure Bettina joined them on all their summer expeditions. She would sit next to him in the car as he drove across the hills, and was thrilled on one occasion when he told her fortune in the tea leaves.

One day, they all decided to wind up their summer activities with a grand party to which, in all innocence, she invited her former lover Bartle. The party was fine: there were prodigal dishes of food, the house was filled with flowers, and the garden with lights as, like shadows, figures wove in and out of the long windows that opened onto the lawn. They moved from house to garden and back again, drinking wine, talking in couples or groups, laughing and dancing to the music played by the old gramophone in the sitting room. At one moment Bettina's eyes met and found Daniel's, who was smiling at her, and she lifted her chin with a new consciousness of delight as she stood in the doorway. But just behind her stood Bartle, his blue eyes glowering under bushy eyebrows, and when later the three of them sat and talked for a while they seemed to have entered a dark and sultry cloud. Bettina, suddenly faced with something she had not foreseen, was invaded by a feeling of helplessness, aware only that, almost by accident, she had unleashed a turbulence she could neither understand nor deal with. And after the party Bartle gave her a lift to town, stopped the car on a heath, and asked her brutal questions about Daniel, trying to make her confess to a love that was so young, so scarcely visible, that she would rather have died than acknowledge it, and had foolishly hoped it might have been allowed to escape notice. But with his intuition aroused, with all the clarity of insight and experience, Bartle had seen the way Daniel looked at Bettina, and watched her unconscious reaction, her evident joy and rapture, which she had thought well hidden. He had fallen prey to jealousy. Bettina was defenceless: idiotically she thought she was to blame. She thought that you ought to know what you felt, even though she found it so difficult to do. She had so little experience, she felt she was walking on quicksands. Incapable of argument, she wept and begged to be forgiven, not realising that she had every right to follow the dictates of her own heart.

After the party Bettina went back again to the house in the country. It had to be scoured from top to bottom, cleaned and tidied, put back as it had been. Daniel came too, and so did Emma, only for a couple of nights. Bettina looked at him sadly, shyly – and her heart leaped again. Surely, as she saw him looking at her, that was what she wanted, a love that was youthful and dangerous because it was equal. He offered more than love and more than chivalry – a life that could be shared together from day to day, without having to make unreal promises, where there could be freedom for each of them and where, above all, she would not be crushed by possession as she had been all her life. With this knowledge, a certain steadiness came back to her, the beginning of an awareness that contained a promise for the future, the only one that – if she held on to it – she would ever need.

The last morning came, and Daniel had to leave early. Having promised to wake him, she knocked on his door. Hearing no sound, she opened it to see his arms entwined with another's. While a voice said, 'Yes, yes, I'm coming,' she saw Emma's head briefly lifted, to disappear once more beneath the sheets. Bettina shut the door and went down to the kitchen. When Daniel eventually came, they sat, one on each side of the table, staring at each other, a pot of coffee between them. Speech froze and silence enveloped her. After a time that might have been a year, but was only long enough for Daniel to swallow a cup of coffee, he rose and kissed her without conviction, mumbling, 'I'm sorry, my dear.' Then he left her. Surely there was something wrong about that – something very, very wrong?

Even at this distance in time, there were some things she deeply regretted and a few she still failed to understand. How feeble she had been, easily pulled from one side to the other. Critical too, without knowing what she was criticising, aping wiser people, shrilly insistent and yet remaining soft and sensitive inside, like a sea urchin. A desperate desire to please took pride of place – feverish to win a smile, unaccountably cast down when she didn't. It was like being on a slippery slope; nothing held fast for long, above all her own feelings. Once, when Jason was away, Maman and the others were talking about his girlfriends, mistresses or whatever they were, and Bettina joined in, her own opinions very definite, very critical. Jason always had more than one girl in tow. Each was dissected, attacked, vulturised, destroyed. Afterwards Bettina found she had amused everyone and was, she thought, being admired. She felt she had done some-thing exceptional. And then, one day, she allowed one of those dreadful sentences to shoot out in Jason's hearing, telling him what she thought of Jane or Alice – and the sentence hung between them, while he took it in, still smiling but, she could see, shocked. He must have seen the whole sequence, must have realised it didn't come only from her. Looking back now she wondered how she could have been so thick, so uncaring. Had she been jealous? Was it jealousy, this forked tongue that leaped out of nowhere? She realised she had gone through a great deal of her life blindly knocking against other people's tender parts, and only afterwards realising her guilt, and suffering a private contortion of spirit. And so she became secretive, hiding things she found it impossible to confess, because they did not belong to her private image of perfection. She was only half a creature, a lame simulacrum, instead of the lovely, spirited Bacchante that Jason and Daniel had wanted her to be.

It was hard to accept being so much younger – she hated it, and it was such a good excuse for them to shove her off, relegate her to the outer circle where nothing mattered and anything she did lost all meaning. She felt accused of being too young, but was not allowed to be anything else. She felt that, had they only treated her as an adult, she would have been one. Even if there had been a few lapses, what would they have signified? She would have learned, and learned quickly, since what else did she need, what else did she want but to plant her bare feet on the stones, to climb the mountain as the others did, slowly finding her own way? Her feeling of never knowing where she was, was due to this uncertainty, and so she behaved frivolously. She could not reach rock bottom where she longed to be; her feet floated in the void. Jason and the others, she knew, wanted her to be firm and solid, but there seemed to be a jinx on it all – she could not manage it.

Perhaps feeling something of the same kind of longing himself, Jason went away to the other side of the world. Those left behind tried to follow him in their minds while he wrote letter after letter describing the strange things that happened to him. Bettina realised clearly that Jason had been trying to learn more, especially about himself; but things didn't come to him easily, and if he sometimes behaved like a clown breaking through a paper hoop, it was in exasperation at himself for having been caught, and allowing himself to be tied down by Maman's silken threads. The family anaesthetised him by obscuring the problem, and by not understanding what he really wanted from life. He was like the man in the story who could not see the valley for the spider's webs that blew in his eyes and bound him hand and foot. Bettina thought she knew now exactly what it had been like for him, and she wished – how she wished – that he had stayed far away, and not come back to the end that awaited him.

War was the end; and all the fear and distrust Bettina had felt as a child seized hold of her again. She remembered the fascination war had always held for Jason, all his childhood games of castles and armies, fortifications and strategies that to her, however beautiful the plans on paper, felt utterly alien. And now, like a plague, war had actually come to a corner of Europe. Striving to make a place for herself, she sat on a committee, and painted a huge poster which was stuck on a hoarding, and she saw and talked to people who had been there. But it was still unreal to her, there was the inevitable layer of cotton wool that interposed itself and prevented her from being shocked, moved and horrified. Her own young life was stronger, it seemed, than death, strong enough to buoy her up in enjoyment, even when her brother was on the battlefield. And yet something inside her, an echo of terror, met actual terror halfway. She knew that Jason would never come back. She felt it was inevitable that she would never see him, or talk to him again. They wrote letters to each other – letters that made her feel younger than ever and, on reflection, inadequate, although she knew this was far from his intention. It must have been very difficult to write from his trench or his truck, feeling himself situated at last in an ultimate reality, something that could neither be avoided nor sidetracked, something hard, vital and strong, where life was expendable and death had to be faced and accepted – how masculine a conception of reality, she could not help thinking, although she could understand his need of it. When the end came, swifter and sooner than she could have imagined, it was nothing – a mere piece of paper, a telegram. Death itself had happened out there, in blood and pain, while for all of them, Maman and herself too, it was the beginning of another pain, bloodless but horrible, one that would never die.

Aurore

Once Upon a Time

For you this is only a story, neither short nor long – something to be read and then forgotten, or at best put away in some dusty corner of the mind, whether or not to be brought out again, only you can tell. But for me it was a real event, or series of events, both the happiest and the most tragic of which took place in that time of anguish and excitement just before the Second World War, and then continued afterwards, when life had shaken itself down to a semblance of tranquillity, to end with the death of a young and brilliant creature standing on the very threshold of life. It was also a moment when I, with no reason or justification, behaved like a snake in the grass, shamefully and disgracefully. In the general disarray my act went unnoticed. I continued to maintain a relationship with my friends to the end, and didn't pay the penalty that should have been demanded of me. But now I never lay down my head at night without asking myself why I behaved so disingenuously, or what provoked such careless and cruel behaviour on my part. And yet, what did I do that was so very shameful? Juliana did not take it that way – and perhaps I am exaggerating. I will tell the story, and allow you to judge for yourself.

Chapter One

I was a very young sixteen when my parents decided to send me abroad to perfect my French. In our family, for some reason, French was preferred to German although I could have learned Italian. This had nothing to do with the language, but with the art, and it was the art that mattered: Italian art was one thing, and French quite another. And of course my parents knew French better than Italian, but I, in spite of having spent part of each year in the south of France, knew practically none at all. I had never made friends with the local children because, as always, we lived well away from the town; although one year I had a governess called Sabine who said, after three months spent with us, that I now knew the whole of French grammar. I was, in fact, as ignorant as could be.

At that time my ignorance did not matter to me. My parents were painters and though they seemed to care only for my happiness it was only happiness connected with the arts that interested them – skin-deep and super-ficial – leaving them free to go in their own direction, and me to snatch as best I could at what they had left behind. But they didn't care whether I achieved anything, which meant that I never sat for an examination, and avoided as much as possible the kind of rewards these tests offered – behaving as if we were above all such considerations, and considered them not worth having. It may seem strange that, brought up in an eminently intellectual atmosphere, I learned only how to feel and not to think. Perhaps unjustly I attribute this to Mother, who did not want me to think, possibly because she intuitively realised that thinking on my part would lead, with time, to my separation from her. That she herself would have totally denied such a thought does not mean there was no truth in it. She took on the attitude of an animal protecting her cubs although, unlike a lioness in the wild, she was incapable of finally rejecting them. But to say she brought me up to feel, is also untrue. I grew up sensitive, but so terrified of my deepest, most personal feelings that I hid them and, since never encouraged to talk, was quite unable to show them. All Mother could do was to give me the feeling that she wanted me to love her and more than anything in the world she wanted some sign to show that she was the only person I really cared for; and because she unconsciously, but all the more remorselessly, betrayed this hunger for love, I could not give her such a sign. Devoured by guilt, I hung round her neck, hoping my failings would not be noticed. It is only now I see that my shyness was a result of her love for me, the love of someone who wants to identify completely with the object of their love, and cannot bear the thought of separation – separation which is another word for death.

Well do I remember those solitary evenings, or rather those evenings *à deux* passed together in front of the stove, neither of us able to talk yet full of weird, totally sincere feelings, champing to come out but too scared both of saying and of hearing that we didn't love each other. I still feel it was her job more than mine, but the devil seemed to be holding her lips tightly shut. This was a very bad sort of education for a girl of fourteen or fifteen, who had just reached the point where anything might happen, and it was particularly bad for me. I had a mother who was anxious to do the right thing and a father I adored; but I could not depend on him since he was partly ruled by my all-controlling mother and very often simply absent, called away by other temptations and less demanding responsibilities. He had not the stuff of fatherhood in him, and could not give me what I needed. Although I had two brothers – they were at that time almost grown up, and lived in a different world from mine – they were kind but rough and oblivious of the feminine point of view.

I was young enough to be full of hope – longing for anything to happen. What it might be I had no idea. Like the fabulous falcon or the tiniest chick, you stand on the edge of the nest, waiting for your wings to be strong enough to carry you into the wide, wide world. In the end, of course, you take your courage in both hands and fly, for there is no other way of finding out. You are courageous but vulnerable, in need of help but without the means of finding it.

I had left school earlier than I should have – partly from boredom and partly because my mother, beautiful and remote, refused either to believe in learning or to leave me to find my own level. I had made one friend who, in a moment of surprising maturity, had entered the grown-ups' world while I had remained a child. I had lost her through no fault of my own but by some mysterious process I did not understand. It was as though she had opened a door on to a shining perspective and then slammed it shut in my face. She may not have been beautiful but she had a power conferred by an early maturity. I wasn't interested in horses, and so had very few friends. I found myself facing a world where there was no one, among my horse-loving companions, who attracted me. My school life had come to an end.

For a time we went to Italy. We knew no one in Rome and, enticing though it was, it turned out in the end to be no more than a brilliant stepping stone to the future, where I decided that mine lay in the theatre, and that I would be an actress. While there we received unexpected news, and returned in haste to London, disturbed but excited also, to find that my elder brother Justin had decided to go to China.

At the other end of the earth and more foreign than Italy, China was in those days, and is perhaps now, as far as you can get from a familiar scene – a place where earth and sky hardly meet, and my mother, while facing a landscape so bleak, found herself making lists and packing shirts in preparation for his long absence. What spelled for him a rich and exciting future, meant for her a period of acute, if exaggerated anxiety, of imagining things she had never seen and never would see, trying to project herself into the life of her favourite son, a life that would, in the end, always elude her. His father, to whom she was married but had tired of long ago, presented her with a smooth, cold face of bland unconcern. They no longer lived together and when, after Justin's departure, they met on Sunday evenings and she read his letters aloud, she knew she could not to look for sympathy. The rest of us, however, listened with interest and an immense desire to understand what was happening to him, his experiences – especially when, for example, he went on an expedition with his friend Yeh to parts of China far off the beaten track. We envied him; while my mother could not conceal her anxiety. Before he left, my brother's preparations resembled those of a Victorian explorer going to the wilds of Africa or

South America: lists of orders, telephone calls to the Army and Navy Stores, the arrival of boxes, parcels, trunks, quantities of books etc. – all this filled our lives and our rooms. My mother's huge studio, full of a painter's belongings and equipment, from easels to stacks of canvases, a model's throne, forgotten still lifes, dead flowers, bruised and rotten fruit, was used by everyone. In spite of being in such a muddle the studio was beautiful, its atmosphere congenial, where we used to entertain our friends at a table covered by dully reflective aluminium set with blue glasses and plates of a thick, leaden white china. I remember my future teacher, Michel Saint-Denis, coming to dinner with his Russian mistress, encouraging me to translate a word of French into English – how happy I was to be asked. How many memories I have of those times long ago. At last the studio was empty, the wastepaper baskets full. The day of Justin's departure had arrived. My mother was melancholy and accompanied Justin to Southampton. The vapour that had fizzed round us evaporated. It was now my turn to be packed up and sent off.

I was too young and too spoiled to see life from my mother's point of view. It was no doubt difficult for her to say goodbye to two of her children at once, even though she could expect to see at least one of them back again soon enough. But we lived at a time when Hitler was threatening our very existence and when we could feel the past palpably slipping away, to be replaced by a future so different as to be unrecognisable. Although I did not realise it, I was part of that future. I was standing on the brink of a nest that was fast disintegrating and from which I would have to fly whether I liked it or not. All of us were blind to a greater or lesser degree and, as though to give us a breathing space, God allowed us a year or two in which to grow, in my case to experience new and so far unimagined things, in the case of my brother and those like him to decide how and where they were going to make their mark.

I returned to London to be thrust into a social whirl, intoxicating and delicious, where I was often tempted to stray out of my depth, but where my innocence, boring though it was, saved me from drowning. The artists' quarter where we lived was not particularly attractive: it was down at heel, depressing in appearance and busy. It was familiar, it was London, but pre-war London, more like a village than it is today. We all knew each other, just as we knew the pubs, cafés and restaurants, and the people who ran them. An indescribable sense of belonging to the same world bound us together where, though I later abandoned it, I could have been supremely happy. It was like a large family party whose gaiety is slightly feverish, where people feel a sense of doom in the air which they accept blindly, fatalistically.

I still didn't know where I was going to. Italy had proved an evanescent, disturbing dream and the obvious alternative was France. There were several different Frances to which I might have gone – all attractive and all imbued with that sense of responsibility and seriousness that struck us then as specially valuable. My mother put out feelers – but, paradoxically, she knew nothing about the theatre, and it was that which attracted me. It is true my father knew Jacques Copeau, who was a great man of the theatre and who spoke perfect French. But his wife was deeply religious and my parents were afraid she would convert me. Oddly enough, however, his nephew, Michel Saint-Denis, came to England at almost the same time and provided a link that I was able to take advantage of when I came back from Paris.

A year or two later I went to see Copeau with my friend Chattie Salaman. As an excuse we took with us a portrait of his beautiful daughter, painted by my mother. He received both us and the picture with exquisite manners, and we sat and talked, dignified, grown-up and shy. He was cardinal-like, with white hair, black eyebrows and magnificent dark eyes. He communicated easily, especially with Chattie – it was as though her orange hair were a set of telephone wires sending out messages in a mysterious code, which I, in my frozen incapacity, could not decipher. The theatre was a thing of the past for him, though, since it had once been his whole life, it was no doubt full of memories. But it was now denuded and empty. The war was coming and the days of his prime were over; nevertheless he was an imposing figure, civilised, experienced, richly encrusted with a past I envied. His nephew, who eventually became my teacher, talked to him and persuaded him to inspect the school at which Chattie and I were pupils. Floundering about in the long tweed skirts we were made to wear, one day I was summoned to shake hands with this tall, imposing figure. It was because I was my father's daughter that secured me that privilege – Copeau remembered him with affection. *'Ah! Ainsi vous voulez être comédienne?'* *'Non,'* said I, betraying my ignorance of the language, *'Tragédienne.'*

This all happened later on though. As I slouched from sun-baked garden into the house at teatime, or came down half-asleep to a late breakfast, Mother would speak of letters she had written or answers she had received from some well-known actor or artist in France, in response to her asking whether they would take me into the bosom of their family. The responses were all negative and we were left high and dry not knowing where to turn, and were only finally saved by Vivienne, a cousin of my father's, half French and half English, who had a good friend, Juliana Deloiseau, who lived in Paris. She and her husband Gilles took in lodgers and, having none at present, would probably take me. Moreover, while Gilles was employed at the Cour des comptes, Juliana was a painter and starting to make a name for herself as an artist. They seemed ideal. My mother wrote to them, and received a favourable answer. She and I set off on a day in September and arrived in Paris, at the Gare du Nord, in the late afternoon, just as it was getting dark.

Chapter Two

Madame Deloiseau's apartment was near the Bois de Boulogne, on the other side of the town from the station. Just before arriving at the Gare du Nord, feeling both bold and guilty, I asked my mother whether I could go alone to meet Madame Deloiseau. I dreaded the smothering effect Mother's presence would have on me at that first meeting. I did not stop to think that Madame Deloiseau would find it strange, or that Mother's feelings would be hurt. A look of surprise crossed her face, austerely beautiful, noble and inhuman and, smiling her understanding, if ironical acceptance, of my desire for independence, she saw me and my luggage into a taxi, and took another to her small, shabby hotel on the left bank, where I suppose she spent the evening alone.

Paris in the rain seemed huge – its numberless lights reflected in the streaming pavements, between the legs of hurrying people whose heads were hidden under black umbrellas. The taxi raced down long avenues of tall grey houses whose façades were punctuated by rows of shuttered windows, always, it seemed, of identical proportions, suggesting an immutable order of existence. My heart raced too, anticipating new friends, new opportunities, new flavours. Excitement replaced the usual lack of self-confidence. Finally, the taxi stopped in front of a high, dun-coloured building on the corner of a cross-roads. I got out of the taxi, pressed the buzzer and the door, of art-nouveau bronze and dimpled glass and immensely heavy, opened grudgingly, allowing the taxi driver to dump my luggage in the entrance hall. An elderly gentleman, on the point of leaving, courteously directed me to the concierge, who instructed me to take the lift to the sixth floor. It was a claustrophobic box rising, it seemed with pain, in a slowly descending perspective of circular stone steps and crimson carpet. The unfamiliar smell, and the sight, on each floor, of other people's front doors, constituted a prelude that did little, on this first occasion, to quench my excitement. Arriving at last under the shadowy ceiling, I rang the bell of a stoutly made, green-painted door. Almost at once I heard the sound of footsteps. After two or three turns of a key the door opened to reveal a middle-aged woman who told me she was Juliana's mother, Madame Eckhardt. Then Juliana herself appeared behind her and welcomed me warmly. She was a dark, sleek-haired woman of medium height, wearing white stockings and low-heeled black slippers like a maja in a picture by Goya. 'I didn't expect you so soon, my dear,' she said. 'Come in. You must be tired.' She spoke English, not with the usual French accent it is true, but with a relish that was far from British.

Straight away she asked, 'Would you like a bath?' But I was much too excited. More than anything else I wanted to talk, to ask questions. So, quickly depositing the suitcases in a corner, Juliana hung up my coat and took me into the living room – a room that still forms a part of my life, so familiar did it become. It was a double-sized room with a folding screen in the centre that could be shut to form a dining room on one side, a studio on the other. At that moment it was open and, by the light of one lamp, looked very large. Tall windows looked down on the street below, but on this autumnal evening the thin, cream-coloured curtains were drawn, and I could not see what proved in the morning to be yet another avenue of blind, sleeping houses. A grand piano, black and shining, stood in one corner, an easel in another. In the centre of one wall was a small stove, and here we sat, one on each side, exactly as I was in the habit of sitting in my mother's studio at home. We plunged deep into conversation, relaxed, uninhibited, as though we had known each other in a past life. 'I will call you Agnès,' she said, 'and you must call me Juliana. We cannot live together all winter on terms of formality.' Her manner was straightforward, friendly and warm. The irony or self-consciousness to which I was accustomed at home, and which seemed to underlie even the simplest statement, here was absent. Soon abandoning the subject of

84

my journey, we talked of music, of favourite composers and what we liked to play. Feeling at ease, I must have stared at her since I remember how she looked that day down to the last detail. Her hair, as I said before, was sleek and parted in the middle, innocent of the attentions of the hairdresser, and caught back in a broad-meshed chenille net. The cleft between her breasts was exposed by the low neckline of her jersey, which was of a rather unpleasant lime green, knitted in tiny stitches. Her waist was slender and her skirt rather long. Beneath it I could see her ankles in their white cotton stockings and her small, black velvet mules. Broad and dignified, with beautiful shoulders, her whole person, including her gestures, was rounded and harmonious. She reminded me of the honeycomb, or the pear hanging on the wall. Surprised at the absence of my mother, she immediately put this right by a proposal to ask her to lunch the following day.

All this time Madame Eckhardt was preparing supper. She was a buxom and elderly lady whose face expressed shrewdness and a suppressed amusement. She was chiefly just an observer of life in the flat, but had a sharp tongue and, on occasion, could interpret remarks that implied a spirit of criticism. Thinking that in my English way I was too timid, she eventually tried to lick me into shape, and would make me do or say things I had hoped to evade. I remember one conversation in the kitchen about the 'facts of life', when she asked me to tell her what everything was called in English! Finally I slunk away, hot and blushing, as she could not believe I did not know.

To return to that first evening with Juliana: we had already started to eat supper, and there had been no mention of Gilles, and I was beginning to wonder when he would come in when I heard the rattle of a key in the lock, and the outer door slammed shut. My heart beat fast, for here was another member of the family to meet – and a man at that! Before he came in Juliana turned to me and said suddenly, 'My husband has a beard,' and we laughed. Then the door opened, and I saw a man walking rapidly up to me. I rose from the table and was confronted by a charming, handsome face with bright, cordial, shining eyes. He looked at me sympathetically and said, '*Bonsoir, Mademoiselle Agnès. Vous n'êtes pas fatiguée?*' '*Non, merci,*' I replied. Then he bent tenderly over Juliana, kissed her on the forehead, and took his place at table. I had already made up my mind that Gilles was a reincarnation of either Mr Rochester or Mr Darcy, my two favourite heroes in literature. On the whole my preference went to Mr Darcy, although I had to allow of course that Gilles was thoroughly French – whatever that meant. Handsome and black-haired, with an Arab tinge about his features, finely modelled and very regular, he was small and rather thin. His clothes were always clean and usually neat, and even when he put on old ones in an effort to deny his city refinement he never looked really dirty or untidy, unlike my brothers at home who wore trousers covered with paint and jerseys frayed at the edges and sometimes with holes in the worst possible places. Though vague and forgetful about his possessions – never knowing where to find anything – Gilles's personal appearance was always presentable. He came from an old-fashioned family where such things were taken for granted. His slight formality relieved me of social anxiety. I knew exactly, more like Jane than Elizabeth Bennet, how to respond to such good manners, although of course my shyness and lack of French often left me blushing.

Soon I was listening rather than talking, trying to follow the conversation between husband and wife. Gilles's behaviour to me was perfect, and for some time I was able to think of him as Mr Darcy. He was very polite, and also very friendly, though frequently preoccupied and unaware of anything save the intricacies of the political situation, or more particularly of his own political intrigues. But more of that later.

After supper I went up to my bedroom – a *chambre de bonne* on a higher floor, which I reached by going out of the back door of the apartment and along an open veranda looking down into the well of the building, up some narrow stairs and along another passage filled with other doors. The room was tiny, containing just a bed, table and wardrobe. I slept in my bedroom but spent no other time there. On that first morning, anxious not to be late, I got up too early, arriving at the locked kitchen door while Juliana was still in bed. Disgusted at my insistent battering, she eventually arrived to unlock it, in dressing gown and slippers, her hair down her back. Leaving me to drink my coffee alone, she went back to bed. This in itself was educational. I learned, although I had no watch, not to appear before nine in the morning.

At home breakfast was a rite, a gentle initiation into the day's work. The table would be laden with a place set for each of us. There was always a shaft of sunlight, a bouquet of flowers, the view through a window into a garden lit with dew. The colours were multiple, soft and soothing. The servants had got everything ready and we had nothing to do. Like the inhabitants of the Palace of the Sleeping Beauty, we might have been drugged.

Here in Paris we sought independently for what we wanted, jostling with each other in the tiny kitchen. That morning Gilles, who had already eaten his breakfast, was preoccupied by a host of commitments which would assail him as soon as he opened his eyes in the morning. He left his coffee and his tartine unfinished, and I would find him, when I appeared, immersed in the newspaper, fingering his beard, a cup of cold coffee on the table. 'Juliana, *chérie*, where are my shoes?' he would call, reluctant to stop reading. 'Which shoes?' a bored voice would reply from the bedroom. 'The new ones, the ones I bought last week, obviously. Where can they be?' From her bed, also reading a newspaper, Juliana would tell him where they were. Once he had his shoes, there would then begin a flustered, anxious hunt for all the necessary papers and letters that he needed for work. Time was short and invariably he would have an important appointment. It was as though the apartment had been invaded by an incipient whirlwind. But the storm would end with a kiss, an '*au revoir, chérie*', and the slam of the front door. When all this took too long he would be compelled to take a taxi and sometimes, opening drawer after drawer, even to hunt for money to pay for it.

Thus Mr Darcy at home was a little different from Miss Austen's hero. But they did have something in common. They were sexually attractive and, each in his own way, conventional and arrogant. There are actually very few of us who are not so, but of this I was unaware at the time. Sometimes I felt dismissed, even before I had opened my mouth, so quick was Gilles; he understood – though often rightly – too soon. He did not give me time to express my own point of view, which made him seem not to care about it. He insisted on my writing to my mother, for instance, once a fortnight while I, feeling that this was my own business, resented his very mild interference. Once he had decided on the matter it was dismissed. Constantly sifting right from wrong, he seemed so sure of himself. Did he never see that he might be wrong? The fact that he seemed to know – as if by divine right – what was right and what was wrong, amazed me, it was so different from the prevailing mode of thought in my own family, which soon came to seem vague and rudderless by contrast. But I squirmed under Gilles's certainties – how could he be so sure of things that, I felt, were the right of the individual to decide for himself?

Attractive, he was also disturbing, and the first young man I had lived under the same roof with who, adult and responsible, steered his own course through life. At home my brothers, though not much younger, were still struggling to free themselves from my mother's possessiveness, whereas the rest of the family, except for me, were only too happy to remain enslaved, to delegate their responsibility, and their power, to such a woman. Mother, like some great liner at sea, was set on her determined course, while on a higher level she exuded generosity and forgiveness amid a flurry of strange uncertainties. Transferred from this arena of subtle manipulation to one of youthful vigour and masculine certainty, I found it hard to adjust my behaviour. Decisions came easily to Gilles. His voice vibrated with youthful authority. His phenomenally quick mind sliced through the pros and cons of my confused thinking to pronounce a perfectly simple, if sometimes unpalatable solution to problems that cropped up.

When I first went to live with Gilles and Juliana, I was both immature and ignorant, but thrilled to be going to live in Paris. I knew its flavour, like the lick of icing from the top of a cake, from having passed through it several times with my family on my way to the south. At least, I thought I knew it though I had been much younger then. I remembered the hotel we had stayed in, in the rue Bonaparte, with its shabby red-carpeted stairs up which I had climbed, like a cat at night, to my room under the eaves. How quiet it had been, and how reassuring – I was welcomed like an old and valued friend, although I was so young. However free and splendid the life outside, the hotel had been stable, and glowed with a quiet pride in the fact that it had not changed for a hundred years.

I had absorbed a vision of the city from my parents, mostly my mother, who spoke of Paris in terms of rapture, implying the delicious irresponsibility of wandering through the streets, along the quais, in and out of the

Louvre, in the footsteps of great artists like Poussin and Ingres, or Picasso and Matisse. This seemed to be what Paris was for; and to sit in cafés and listen to brilliant conversation quite different from anything to be found in London. To stare into shop windows that were miracles of dust-laden, elaborate arrangement, and with a screen behind which I could imagine a white-haired, sharp old lady, guarding her treasure like a spider in its web. And people hurried past you in the street, full of secret energy and purpose, which set them apart from the vacantly staring tourists. Merely to sit and watch was an education in itself.

But though it was like a rich embroidery, full of exciting and subtle colours, Paris was at the same time no more than a set of words and images to which I had become accustomed. Like pieces of furniture which I stumbled against in the dark. Familiar, but stale. As yet I hardly knew what my true interests were: they lay in the future, unacknowledged, furtive and secret. Like any young girl I was interested in the clothes in the shop windows, and also those things that, as yet unknown, I felt were waiting for me with the discovery of freedom and the strange new self that was to be found in this fascinating and seductive town. My first ten days passed quickly. I was becoming used to the morning *angoisse* and Gilles's late return in the evenings when, suddenly, he had to go to

England on business. We were reduced to a family without our man.

In the morning Juliana and I would do our shopping in the rather forbidding and gloomy streets of the *quartier*. She walked with a stately step in small shoes with low heels and swaying skirts. I went with her to the market – a large square within five minutes' walk, which, on two or three mornings a week, would be full of trestle tables, loud-voiced men and women wrapped in grey shawls, their red fingers protruding from mittens, weighing fruit and vegetables, cutting down hanks of sausages, handling slippery fish on slabs of broken ice, or wrapping up butter and cheese in tiny quantities and handing it to some stout gentleman or fragile old lady in exchange for carefully counted coins. Twenty minutes from the centre of Paris, they might have been in any provincial town. Jokes were rife, everyone knew each other, every housewife – quite often impersonated by her husband – had her favourite merchant, and every tradesman knew how to talk to his client.

On the whole, the *quartier* was *triste* and dull, the shops uninteresting, the houses ugly, huge and forbidding, sheltering heaven knows what abysmally conservative families. Juliana knew no one in the district – she and Gilles had chosen to live there because the air was purer.

To me, at that time, this seemed of little importance. I was sad they did not live in the fifth or sixth arrondissement, where life would have been much gayer and more exciting. But they were not rich enough, and to Juliana this would have meant effort, probably wasted. Friends, social life, hospitality, yes – but no café life, and constantly dashing here and there simply to please other people who, as likely as not, would leave you in the lurch. True, Juliana did not really like Paris, but she was in love with Gilles who was committed to a life there to earn his living and who, if the truth were told, did not much like the countryside.

And yet, had she lived in the rue Bonaparte, Juliana would have looked more normal, or, rather, her own particular style would have been appreciated. Here in Auteuil, the strength of her personality was somehow wasted. Full of nostalgia for her past, her girlhood in Provence, her English lessons with Madame Eckhardt's friend Dorothy, her memories of coming to England during the war, her father whom she adored; she was blind to the merits of the sophisticated and successful. Paris had been a dead-end, a disappointment. Here she had said goodbye to her youth, and felt occasional forebodings as to what might lie ahead. She had no children, work was the only solution. She missed the sun, the shade of the olive trees and the soothing society of Dorothy, who had taught her to love the poetry of Donne and

Ben Jonson, and the novels of Dickens. It was here in Paris that she had started life as a pianist – a career that terminated in a single performance, and was thereafter relegated to a painful memory – yet it was here too that she met Gilles for the first time.

Much later I learned that she had been in love with someone else to whom she was engaged, but who had climbed in through her bedroom window and tried to rape her. This event had produced a nervous breakdown, from which she was only rescued by her mother's devotion and Gilles's perseverance. Now she never spoke of it and, it was hoped, had forgotten it. She had, at all events, been very attractive, and in my eyes was so still.

Juliana was at this time about twenty-eight, twelve years older than I was. Although culturally French to the core, by blood she was a mixture. Her mother was half French and half Spanish. This, I thought, accounted for Juliana's exotic moody quality, her frequent disinclination to act – either to find Gilles's shoes or to go out shopping. It was a kind of lazy power she exercised when she felt so inclined. Her broad, low forehead and level green eyes glowed with warmth, and I was fascinated by her wide, sensuous mouth which, never disguised with lipstick, expressed such generosity. '*Ma petite Agnès*,' she would say when we got home, dumping the laden basket on the kitchen table, 'put all this away, and we will have some music – and some coffee.' She walked, swaying gently, into the living room and, sitting down with a sigh, put her elbows on the red-checked tablecloth. 'Why don't you play some Bach, and I will go on with my painting.' And while I sat down to practise the third prelude of the 48, she would fetch her palette and brushes and push her old easel into the middle of the room, and paint a still life of purple anemones in a turquoise jar. Her gestures were both expressive and self-contained, rounded off before they became ragged or awkward, and although she had something earthy about her, a bucolic breadth and freedom, she also had dignity, a sense of style.

In conversation she was slow and emphatic, listening carefully to what the other person had to say, and then stating her own idea methodically from beginning to end, even when interrupted by Gilles. He was deeply in love, seduced not only by her personality, but because she was an artist and could create things that he was incapable of making. Her personality was strong and her conviction absolute. Emphasising each point as she proceeded, she did not seem to care very much what anyone else thought of her. Extremely well read both in French and English literature, she was often witty and amusing, and would sometimes laugh with abandon, throwing herself backwards in her chair and slapping her knees with her hands. At such moments the scene reminded me of one of those Flemish interiors of the seventeenth century, with a handsome, if not too refined cook, laughing at some joke in the kitchen.

Chapter Three

It was around that time that Vivienne, my second cousin once removed, telephoned and asked Juliana and me out to lunch, probably prompted by my mother, who undoubtedly wanted to know how I was getting on. Vivienne, half French and half English, divided her time between the two countries and was then on her way to join her parents in the south. We met in a large old-fashioned brasserie somewhere near the rue des Saints Pères, where I, much to Vivienne's scarcely concealed annoyance, could find nothing to eat. I suppose this was a misguided way of drawing attention to myself. Finally, however, I ordered a dish that needed special preparation, and while waiting for it, observed these two old friends, who had spent most of their childhood together. I had expected intimacy, visible affection – but Vivienne's mouth was pulled down at the corners and Juliana's natural warmth was veiled. Was it only Vivienne's disapproval of my spoiled behaviour, or was she preoccupied by the long journey that lay ahead of her and the arrival in a different landscape and a different climate? Seeing that effort was needed, she pulled herself together, suggesting somehow that she understood more than she could say, and that much wisdom and benevolence were discreetly hidden behind her constant irony. Elegant, thin and chinless, she was liable to look dour and gloomy in repose but, nudged into life, her face utterly changed. Her almost black, almond-shaped eyes glowed with life and her tongue produced some sour-sweet comment which, as often as not, provoked our laughter. A true intellectual, her intelligence, rather than her emotions, ruled her life. Immensely articulate, she seldom failed to give pleasure, although often of an acidulated variety, particularly when she regaled us with gossip about her famous friends. Her standards of discrimination were finely graded and, when those in the limelight failed to pass the test, she could be severe, although never humourless – laughter saved her from being nasty.

Though possessed of a wit that could freeze the blood, Vivienne was essentially both good and charming. She must have presented something of a challenge to admirers; yet she was by no means unattractive. Vivienne had spent a couple of weekends with us at home in England. She was happy to devote herself to our theatrical enterprises; my father called her a '*jolie laide*', my brothers fell in love with her, or perhaps, more accurately, she with them, and she was very fond of my mother, who admired her watercolours.

I have a feeling that, although she said nothing so explicitly, Vivienne was secretly critical of Juliana's painting. It was so obviously religious, whereas Vivienne and her family were outright agnostics. Her watercolours were fresh and charming – but they carried no message, except one of pleasure in life as she found it. Vivienne probably thought that there was a certain pretentiousness in Juliana's pictures, with which she found it hard to sympathise. But Juliana, though silent on the subject, did actually believe in God. A few years earlier she had found some little books that were clear on the topic, one never talked about in her family, so that her father, who appeared to my brother like a saint, was actually an agnostic or unbeliever, while Juliana, adoring him, also adored God. Although she said little about it, it was natural for her. One of her teachers was Vivienne's father, Simon, to whom she listened devoutly, and, though his painting was very different, he admired her gift. Thus the friendship between these two old friends consisted of many things they never talked about, which went some way to explain the feeling of unease.

It was through Vivienne that Gilles first got to know Juliana. Vivienne had met him in Menton as, overworked and suffering from the effects of living in an unsympathetic household, he was recovering from a severe illness. She invited him to meet her parents, and as he was entering the house, Juliana was leaving it, accompanied by a gruff and implacable Simon. Gilles was left alone with Dorothy and Vivienne in the drawing room, half his attention monopolised by the shy young girl he had brushed past in the passage. It was she who one day later on invited him to go for a walk with her, taking him much further over the hills than his strength then allowed – and it was there, on the pine-scented, rocky slopes looking down on the sea, that, a few weeks later, he proposed to her.

As Gilles regained his health, it became clear that he would have to return to Paris, and now that he was responsible for a wife, a friend found a job for him in the Cour des comptes. He was younger than most of his colleagues – but this was no drawback. I never knew exactly what he did there, only that his job was largely unpolitical; it was, I was told, more like the House of Lords than anything else. It suited Gilles to a certain extent, but the livelier part of his mind was attracted to politics.

I don't know why the memory of that meal remains so distinct in my mind. Nothing special happened, although no doubt both Juliana and I were amused by Vivienne's gossip. Of course underneath her apparent severity there was a lot of generosity and she would soon return to her life of contemplation and security in the south, where she would wake the following morning to the sight of the ochre-coloured houses and the bunches of grapes waiting to be cut from the vines. Perhaps Juliana envied her. When we left her on the Quai Voltaire, she said to me, 'Dearest Agnes, come and stay with us whenever you like, providing you can tear yourself away from Juliana.' Then we took the Métro back to our suburban domesticity, and the regular habits of a quiet family.

For me it was secretly thrilling. Perhaps Juliana imagined that I would be out all day learning about Paris, absorbing culture, seeing friends, going to classes of one kind or another like other lodgers; but she must have soon realised that, having neither friends nor work, I was scared to go too far. It was not simply that I was ignorant of the world, but I seemed to have been made without defences. I was like a day-old lamb wandering through a forest of bears or wolves, owing my survival to what is generally called innocence but is really, I think, the blindest egotism. I was not exactly stupid, and yet Juliana must have wondered where I could have spent my first sixteen years without becoming a little wiser. I think it must have given her an even more exalted idea of my mother, who must surely have been very extraordinary not to have insisted on a more realistic view of life in the jungle.

But Juliana, motherly and concerned though she was, did not try to change me. She spared me those narrow, exemplary lessons that are supposed to teach the young how to shoot, how to grow into the same species of plant as the teacher; she took it for granted that I wanted something better than that. On the practical level, she was warm, decisive and instructive. But apart from showing me how to cook certain dishes or how to wash or iron in the way she preferred, she lifted our relationship on to an altogether more exalted plane, expecting me to learn by inference, by reading the classics, by coming into contact with art, music and theatre – anything, in fact, that represented thought and emotion of the most vibrant and stimulating character.

Gilles returned from London and our life resumed its previous pattern. I began to note the difference between Gilles and Juliana, his rapier-like decisiveness, her slow deliberation. Both witty and cultured, it was Juliana who occupied the centre of the scene, Gilles the wings. When Juliana was talking seriously she disliked interruption, but Gilles always broke in, fired into disagreement or wishing to qualify her statements. His manner was the opposite of hers – quick and concentrated, intense but rather as though, with each sentence completed, he had finished with it. Juliana, on the contrary, talked as though she were building a tangible structure, and when she paused, you could almost see it sitting on the table. She not only had the gift of self-expression, but a considerable amount of histrionic ability.

There was no one like her for telling a story, with her marvellous sense of timing, her witty, common-sense comments and her splendid dénouements. Her laughter would ring out – she was so impressively sure of herself, so right and true in what she said, that I simply melted in her warmth and geniality. But though I melted, I also hardened in the more primitive belief that, if I absorbed enough, my whole nature would benefit, much as the savage who eats his neighbour.

Juliana was the rock, the foundation stone of the family. On all practical matters, she was the only authority. Gilles was no good as 'the man about the house': he was incapable of mending anything or making any practical decision, and could not write his ordinary business letters without a discussion with Juliana. He was so forgetful and he could never be relied on to turn off the gas when they went out for the evening.

Gilles could never sit still and enjoy a drink, basking in the sunshine. Such simple pleasures passed him by – and although he would sometimes laughingly condemn himself for such an attitude and understand theoretically that he was missing much that other people enjoyed, he had no idea of the burden he imposed on Juliana by his restlessness. She had of course long ago accepted the fact that, not only was he incessantly on the hop, but that she could get no help from him in practical matters.

When she wasn't too annoyed with him she would express her feelings with a deep sigh and a resigned tone of voice. She never laughed at Gilles, although she could be bitter at times; I think she very rarely laughed at anybody, which was one of the reasons why I felt such confidence in her. She took everyone else as seriously as she took herself which, especially in the case of some of their protégés, was sometimes more than they were worth. But although Gilles continued to forget, or misunderstand, their affection, their passion for each other survived. When his work kept him at the office, Gilles would usually telephone. One evening, the phone did not ring and Gilles did not appear. We ate our supper with only one subject for conversation: where was Gilles? The evening was fine, and Juliana hung out of the window, gazing at each taxi as it approached the building – none of them contained Gilles, and the tension grew. 'Agnès, I recommend you never marry anyone like Gilles!' At last we heard the sound of the lift, the heavy door clicked, and Gilles presented himself, completely unaware of our anxiety and longing only for a moment's quiet in which to eat his supper. But Juliana wouldn't look at him. To her at that moment, exacting punishment was her deepest need – or was it simply enjoyment of a well-worn, classic drama? Gilles was compelled to go through with it and beg for forgiveness to have any rest, or be allowed to put a forkful of food in his mouth. They were so immersed in themselves and each other that I stared without embarrassment. It was as good as being at the theatre – they acted so well! At last it was over, and, for once, we went immediately to bed.

The truth was, Gilles led a double life. His work as a senior civil servant bored him. His real commitment was to politics and, in particular, to editing a small weekly newspaper. It was this that would sometimes occupy him until two in the morning, pacing up and down his room while smoking a pipe, writing, reading, discussing, telephoning, immersed in theories, making decisions, devoured by a sense of time running out. He had no doubt that what he was doing was all-important, absolutely necessary – above all he wanted his small voice to be heard in the wilderness – but how much could he do, how much could he achieve? A fever possessed him (in the light of which he foresaw the war that was to come) and he found it impossible to relax, or to adjust to the speed of ordinary human beings.

Whatever his shortcomings, in one respect he was quite un-ordinary. He was utterly unworldly, unambitious, and had no desire to become rich and powerful. His attitude to such things was austere, pure to the point of utter self-forgetfulness and lack of egotism, and he possessed a willingness to admit he was in the wrong, which was thoroughly disarming. Among his peers he was the only truly disinterested person – and certainly the main inspiration – the only one whose integrity was beyond all doubt, a fact that became apparent long after I had ceased to live with them.

It was perhaps for this quality that Juliana most loved him, and that allowed her to accept his incessant restlessness, his exasperating incapacity to forget his work and enjoy a glass of wine or caress unthinkingly a cat or some other animal. Meals were forced interludes for him, the only justification the conversation, rather than the excellence of the cooking. And although he would condemn himself, laughingly, for such an attitude, half realising what he was missing, the devil had him in tow, and he could do nothing about it.

Chapter Four

I still continued to think of Gilles as a romantic hero. Only gradually did he sink to the level of an ordinary human being. I was constantly desirous of his good opinion, but the first time he really took any notice of me, apart from politeness, was when I helped Juliana – who was not feeling well – and I heard him say to her on my leaving the room: '*Elle est gentille, cette petite, hein?*' I was delighted and began to understand that even Mr Darcy could be quite human, and I eventually became very fond of him. Of course one may think that Mr Darcy is a thin, unreal character in the book, but Gilles's spiritual sympathies were so narrow that he too had a quality of unreality, especially later on when he was unhappy. Morally speaking he was conventional, and full of the *idée reçue*. He was so constantly engrossed by purely intellectual subjects, and had so little interest, comparatively speaking, in the more sensuous and enjoyable aspects of life, that he was inclined to disregard the importance that other people gave them. He would work out an emotional problem as though it were a piece of arithmetic and when he reached the conclusion would simply say: 'That is what so and so must feel – there is no other possibility.' He was not entirely without a sense of humour, though this relative lack did make him difficult to live with. Although he seldom made jokes himself, he enjoyed other people's, and was often made to laugh at himself with very good grace. My chief employment socially was to distract him, when ever possible, from his political preoccupations and tease him a little into humanity. But although he liked this, and even enjoyed being teased, he was always nervous, always ready to jump up and pace the room, talking incessantly.

Coming back from a piano lesson one day, I found a swarthy, dark-haired young man in the apartment. He was introduced to me as Bruno, a protégé of Juliana's. He had been on holiday when I arrived, but now resumed his part in our family life, and seemed to be regarded with the same deep affection reserved for a favourite and trusted sheepdog. Where he came from and what work he did, I only found out later. I was probably not very interested, but I was also shy, and vacillated from on the one hand a longing to ruffle my fingers through his plumes of black hair, and a slight repulsion for his unshaven cheeks. He also often smelled of garlic, and blew his nose very loudly on a red cotton handkerchief. He was without social graces, but had kind, liquid black eyes, and treated me with a sort of clumsy gallantry that I learned to take in my stride.

109

Often he would turn up in the evening, not having eaten anything all day, and Juliana would give him a piece of sausage and some bread and cheese, and then sit and listen to any gossip he had unearthed. As soon as she was bored, she would cut him short and tell him to go and find Gilles in his study. Once there Bruno seldom appeared again before I went to bed (being a great sleeper, I often went early), but sometimes he sat awkwardly in the living room on a chair at the table, munching and listening to Gilles, who talked as though thinking aloud, very likely also nibbling a crust of dry bread while striding up and down the room. It was obvious that nothing existed for him except what was going on in his head. At such moments I never listened to him, since if there ever was an apolitical animal, I was it. Politics always failed to stimulate, motivate or interest me. I had listened to a lot of impassioned political talk at home, and detested the loud voices, the red faces, the almost uncontrollable emotions, reacting like a frightened mouse caught at the entrance to its home. I could not make out what the politicians were up to, what the connection was with our daily lives. I could not even remember their names. So I found Gilles's conversation largely unbearable, monotonous and one-sided, addressed to Bruno as though he were a wooden post set there with the express purpose of provoking Gilles to fresh bursts

110

of eloquence. Bruno, his forehead wrinkled with concentration, listened loyally. But his answers, instead of putting the desired end to the argument, often proved that he had got hold of the wrong end of the stick and so was compelled to listen to another vehement explanation. It was no wonder that, in the end, he always agreed with Gilles.

I suppose it was in order to write down these torrents of words that Juliana, or perhaps even Bruno himself, had the idea that he should learn shorthand. Life already seemed hard enough, but now a new burden was added. Each evening he brought exercises with him to learn or copy before his next lesson, and would sit at the table we used for everything, gruffly sighing over mysterious black marks. Juliana would encourage him in a motherly way; while saying at the same time that she would have nothing to do with it, she would look on from a distance, as he learned this new art alone and unaided. But night after night it was actually she who goaded him to his corner after supper, making sure he produced his notebook. Occasionally exasperated by his slowness, she would say: 'Bruno, *mon petit*, if you want to be serious in life, you will have to make an effort. Come on, do a bit more.' So Bruno would blow his nose, and start on a new page of figures. Whatever made him slow, it was not lack of seriousness. I felt at moments that it was an excess of this quality that prevented him from making faster progress.

Meanwhile Juliana was, of course, always painting. It was not long before I sat for my portrait, a common hazard in those long-ago days when I was living with a painter. But again, how different the atmosphere here from the studio at home in England, where the scene was set so carefully to produce a situation where everyone was happy, including the model, where the cool tones of my mother's voice seemed to soothe everyone and create the necessary calm, dream-like concentration that enclosed and protected them; only to be broken, on occasion, by the cook's coming to ask for orders, or the gardener wondering whether he should pick the plums.

But in Paris I stared at the strange dinginess that surrounded us: the greyish, cream-coloured walls, the heavy, coarse furniture, the colourless curtains and chair covers. How could Juliana accept such a utilitarian, depressing atmosphere? Lack of money would have been the answer, but it did not hold water. I knew many other people, such as Vivienne, for example, who, with purses as small, managed to show a sensibility to their surroundings that seemed to leave Juliana indifferent. She was sensuous, but she was also austere. In her presence I used to feel there were deeper, more serious things to think about – Juliana's emotions, though never superficial, were near the surface. For good or ill these emotions underlaid her paintings – nothing to do with the sweet simplicities of decoration, they betrayed a certain violence, and were far from the cool detachment of my parents' art, my only source of comparison. If I thought of my mother's inexplicable decision, suddenly welling up from unknowable depths, to paint some red-hot pokers, or to change the aspect of her bedroom, say, painting the walls, re-hanging the pictures, choosing or re-designing a new bedspread, as though each choice were as important as adding the last line to a sonnet, I was struck with the difference, rather than the similarity between artists. And it was Juliana's personality rather than her art that seduced me.

Juliana painted standing in the middle of her living room, liable to interruption by the plumber or electrician who, if they came, were treated to a display of formality and to whom she said 'Monsieur' so often it was as though they had been transferred on to the stage of the Comédie Française. They usually responded perfectly. All that was needed was lace ruffles and plumed hats instead of adjustable spanners and boiler suits. But as they hammered or wrenched she continued to enjoy herself, momentarily unaware of their existence. I found her lack of false gentility congenial. As she put on her apron and took up her brushes, it was as though she said:

113

'Here I am, doing what I like best. If you disapprove because my house is shabby and I am covered in paint, I couldn't care less. I simply want to be left alone to enjoy myself.'

In those days many of her canvases were large. Some of them hung on the walls – unframed, unvarnished statements – and, in spite of their size and their adumbration of faceless quasi-biblical figures in various shades of russet and brown, recreated the ancient world of Jesus and his disciples. Sitting there, facing her, while she brushed me in with large bold strokes, I thought more of her than of her pictures. There seemed to be two of me, one physically present, and another, quivering with mute admiration.

When not overwhelmed by work, Gilles would spend long moments in front of his wife's paintings. Placing them one in front of the other, in the best light, he would dissect, analyse, and pronounce judgement, enthusiastic about one, less so about another. Finally, with an uncompromising 'This one is undoubtedly the best,' he would puff on his pipe, wave his hand and leave for his study. I was surprised when I found he wrote art criticism – but so it was. One day he paid me the compliment of giving me his article to read on Seurat. I was impressed, and therefore less surprised when, much later, I realised he wrote poetry as well. As was perhaps to be expected, his poems were short, concentrated and intensely intellectual, although, at the same time, they stemmed from strong emotion. It was an emotion that, I felt, having been suppressed, was hard to reveal. Again, though I was never sure I properly understood them, I was impressed by their perfection. His personality evidently contained depths of which he himself was only partly aware, and which, obviously, he didn't like thinking about.

Chapter Five

Meanwhile an independent existence began to sketch itself out for me. I got the hang of the various *quartiers* of Paris, of its cinemas, its boulevards, the better known cafés and art galleries, the river, the churches, the bridges and the statues. This knowledge remained pretty superficial because I had no French friends to give me an inside view, but I did take in the 'feel' of things, and an increasing knowledge of the language helped. Sometimes I would take the bus and go back to the only *quartier* I did know, and moon about on the quais, looking for fashion plates or books of poetry, or I would go to the Quai de la Mégisserie and look at the animals in cages or fish in aquariums or, getting bored of this, would go and indulge my fancies of dressing beautifully by wandering about the Trois Quartiers or the Galeries Lafayette. None of this, however, was very satisfactory. Occasionally I went with Juliana to an art exhibition or to the cinema or the theatre, where I saw both Copeau and Jouvet, the latter dark and malevolent, while Copeau was tremendously dignified as the priest in *Much Ado About Nothing*, holding Hero in his arms as she faints when Don Pedro swears she is no virgin. Here I saw him as I wanted him to be – a father figure, noble and detached, but I, unfortunately, was only in the audience and not on the stage.

I waited, as it were, in the wings, hoping that something would happen before much more time had elapsed as, indeed, it eventually did. But first, as I have said, Juliana painted my portrait, telling me how Simon had painted Vivienne's in deathly silence which gave her an expression of sulky boredom. Not that Juliana talked to me much. '*Ma chère Agnès, assieds-toi là.*' And in next to no time she had set up her easel, and was drawing me in charcoal while I listened to stories of her father who, though still alive, had become a figure of the past for her. I knew he had set himself apart: there was something a little saint-like about him, a little self-conscious.

As I said, Juliana's paintings were large and religious in feeling. But there were also nudes, and small canvases of flowers in bright colours, although she didn't paint still lifes of objects on tables, as in Morandi or Chardin. It was obvious that Juliana herself felt happiest painting these amorphous, religiously echoing pictures where the figures, though without faces, reminded me of her parents or herself – but there was little colour in them, only supposed emotion, and it was difficult to see how they could be fitted into any domestic setting or how anyone could buy them. All artists need to talk to someone about their work and although, up to a point, Juliana could talk to Gilles, his precise and meticulous words left her feeling misunderstood. She needed someone with another point of view, with whom she was less familiar. I do not think Juliana ever found such a person, but in the end it hardly mattered because this gap was filled by her daughter.

Before Madame Eckhardt returned home I had a chance to see what was, for me, a new kind of relationship between mother and daughter. Culturally, Madame Eckhardt was more limited than Juliana and had never, for example, thought of learning a foreign language – but this did not prevent them from understanding each other. I thought the explanation for this was that Juliana had grown up, and the generation gap was therefore smaller; indeed one might think that the wind was blowing the other way, and that, with a more audacious view of life and herself, Juliana had long outstripped her mother. My own experience was of people never being happy, yet being simply what they were; they all wanted to be something else, either instead of, or as well as their normal self. But Madame Eckhardt saw life differently. She had started as a singer, and still had a magnificent, if slightly hollow voice, to which she would occasionally give tongue when wandering about the living room, or sitting bolt upright in her chair at the table – she was justifiably proud of it. She then met Jean, her cousin who was later to become her husband, and she was absolutely happy to be a devoted wife and mother. Jeanne Eckhardt was an important figure in all our lives. She had her own reservations and mute criticisms of course, and although it was still discernible that she had been a beauty, she now had a double chin and a thick, solid figure. But she was respected by everybody, amused though they sometimes were by her old-fashioned ideas. Even in this role she was limited but it did not seem to worry her. Though never intimate with her, I grew to like her and even to be comforted by her presence. Nonetheless, I was secretly glad when Madame Eckhardt left to go back to her husband, holding the fort in their tiny house on the shore of the Mediterranean. Madame Eckhardt too was glad to go, I felt. She had taken no part in the joys of Paris, bringing with her a strong flavour of the simple, country life, which, I imagined, she always carried about with her like an invisible hold-all, which held within it everything essential to her happiness.

It was well before the First World War that Jean and Jeanne had met Vivienne's parents, Dorothy and Simon. They had become mutually devoted. It was Dorothy whom Juliana came to love most, and eventually learned English from her and developed an admiration for the Jacobean poets, allowing her to enjoy much that was denied to her parents. Thus, even when very young,

119

Juliana was admired by a whole group of people, who found it hard to understand why she left them to go and live far away in Paris.

My understanding of politics was both hazy and lazy. But a 'something in the air' became clearer to me from listening to, or overhearing the conversations that took place between Gilles and Bruno. They were concerned by the menace of war, which seemed to be getting closer, but about which I knew very little. I had shut my ears to it because I found it so frightening and only knew what my old nurse had told me, or what I had gathered from my brothers who, to my amazement, found it exciting. But there was another threat, more local this time – a sort of political disintegration that Gilles feared and was standing out against. His newspaper was called *Vigilance*. It was a voice, intended to bring people to their senses before it was too late. He was very committed, running it single-handedly, staying up until the small hours dictating to Bruno, who frequently got into trouble because he was too slow. Gilles, his mind entirely occupied with this idea, spared no one – even Juliana was brushed out of the way. Had she not consented with her whole being to what he was doing, I felt it might have been a painful situation. Now, when Gilles came home, it seemed as though it was only from politeness that he sat down to supper with us, he was so consumed by his longing to return to work. He spent every possible moment composing articles for the newspaper and discussing political matters over the telephone. I was impressed by his single-minded enthusiasm and devotion – although the details of his opinions meant nothing to me – and it helped me, later, to understand the danger that he was in. For the moment, however, I kept myself apart, and looked on with more interest in his frame of mind than in his politics.

The leaves in the streets had disappeared. Autumn was over and winter had arrived. One day, Juliana admitted to excitement. 'Come, Agnès,' she said, 'let us go and look. There is a studio for rent just opposite.' And there, in a garden behind an iron grille at the end of a court-yard, was a large, isolated studio. There was nothing in it but a stove, the smell of damp wood and autumn leaves. Juliana had only to beckon a carpenter and a plumber and almost overnight everything was renovated, installed and arranged to her satisfaction. Now she would work, have time, peace – and a place of her own. No telephone messages for Gilles, no endless conversations with her mother-in-law, no demands from the concierge to interrupt her. And the huge space, the arched ceiling, the wooden walls like those of a chalet in Switzerland, were so delightful. We talked it over and agreed that she had done the right thing, however costly it was, however daring. She installed her easel and painted away to her heart's content. I bought bread and fruit and in the middle of the day we would eat a sandwich and throw the wrapping paper away – no washing up, no chores except the occasional caress of a hairless broom on the wooden floor to sweep away the crumbs and the little balls of hairy dust that came from nowhere.

It was here that she started painting a large picture of a man leaning over a wall as if looking for something he had lost, in an obviously Provençal landscape. A tree hung over him and there was a village faint in the distance. Juliana became fascinated by this picture, where the man did not look either like her father or Gilles and was therefore a pure product of her inspiration since it was impossible to imagine Juliana in love with anyone else. She worked at it hard – but never finished it. I too was riveted, but disappointed. I never knew what was in her mind, and would watch while she painted with immense concentration, yet the painting never developed.

And then we would have a grand fête in the evenings. We would play 'Le Chaland qui Passe' on the gramophone over and over again. Gilles would come home, and we'd eat our evening meal in picnic fashion, feeling free and irresponsible. How gay we were, how easily pleased! How serious was Juliana about her painting, and how much Gilles wanted her to paint a masterpiece, and even more that she should be happy.

I was thrilled by the thought that at Christmas I would be seventeen. There were presents and we danced, me in the arms of Bruno, Juliana in the arms of Gilles. Outside the studio the chestnuts had made their yearly contribution of yellow leaves, which rustled round my feet as we walked back to the apartment at midnight. Bruno slept on the sofa, and in the morning we breakfasted together in the knowledge that Gilles would not have to go to his office. But the magazine took up more and more of his time. His dictations were endless. Juliana, stepping into his study in her low-heeled shoes, brought him and Bruno cup after cup of black coffee. One day it even transpired that Gilles, unpractised in sport or games, was going to a shooting gallery to learn how to shoot a revolver. I was told later that he was afraid of a group called Action Française, and thought a coup d'état was possible, and he might need to defend himself.

Life went on in much the same way for what seemed quite a long time. I had flu and was allowed to sleep downstairs in the sitting room, which gave me a still more intimate feeling of being part of the family. Looking back I can think of nothing painful that happened there, and was surprised when I remembered a day – I think only one, but one of incredible length – when I could not stop crying. I came down to breakfast in tears, and no matter what Juliana said to me I only produced more tears, with no kind of explanation. I was like a tap that someone had forgotten to turn off, simply running, flooding everything, from handkerchiefs to nightgown – even my hair got wet. And once I had recovered, then Juliana had a mysterious illness and had to stay in bed for most of every day. I did the shopping and sometimes a little cooking. Bruno made himself useful. Gilles continued to work, but would come back earlier in the evenings and sit for a long time on Juliana's bed, gossiping.

Eventually, Juliana said to me one day: '*Ma petite Agnès*, I think I am going to have a baby. That is what is making me so tired – and I must be careful not to lose it. I think, as she's asked you, it would be a good thing if you went to stay for a time with Vivienne in the south, and then, perhaps, with my mother and father.' I was thrilled by the news that Juliana was going to have a baby; and I loved the idea of seeing more of this France that I found so fascinating, although I knew it so little.

So, quite soon, I set off on the journey that Vivienne had taken months ago, travelling by night to arrive in the early dawn, in a new landscape, an atmosphere welcome and refreshing after Paris. I had a cup of coffee and arrived at Menton, to be met by Vivienne who, as she didn't drive, had hired a taxi. We climbed a steeply curving road for several kilometres, arriving at last outside a modest-looking house on a steep slope, facing the sea and the hazy, pearly coast. Round the house was a garden, bathed in the warm sun of the south, full of orange and lemon trees and small, bright blue irises nestling in the grass.

There is not much to say about my relation to Vivienne's family – I knew them as one knows the furniture in someone else's house. They were exceedingly kind, but too old for me, so that I was always on my best behaviour and I was, in a way, happy eventually to move up the hill to stay with Jeanne and her husband who were not only a bit younger than Vivienne's parents but also less intimidating.

Yet I saw little of French life with them; indeed neither Jean nor Jeanne ever invited anyone to the house while I was there; although I later realised that friends, who stayed with Simon and Dorothy, would often find their way up the hill to see Jean's pictures, and to talk to him about painting. But as far as I could see neither Jean nor Jeanne needed visitors or companions, being everything to each other. Some of his favourite pictures were hung on the walls and the decor was simple and pure and, I suppose, suited Jean's personality – but my dream of getting to know more of the French proved rather a mirage. I saw less of them than I had in Paris, and even less than when I had been staying with Simon and Dorothy, who at least had distinguished friends to lunch to whom I was introduced. One of them, Roger Martin du Gard, a writer, took my fancy and even paid me some attention, while Matisse, who was an old friend of Simon's, looked at the watercolour that I happened to be doing, and pronounced it '*pas mal du tout*'.

I read a good deal and roamed for hours round the countryside. The cottage was outside the village and I could walk for miles without meeting anybody, only perhaps a herd of sheep and their shepherd. Jeanne would cook delicious meals and I was careful to eat up every crumb, having heard the story of how shocked she was in England during the war to see plates taken away with food still on them – which might have saved the poor from starvation if eaten in Belgium.

I would of course have loved to stay in France for the sense of freedom I felt when not living in the family circle where, though I was loved, I was never allowed out of sight. When I helped Jeanne in the kitchen or when I walked out alone on the hills, it was all part of my French experience, and I would have liked to go further and deeper. But my parents could not afford it, and I was not independent enough to branch off on my own and get a job, so I was condemned to treat this as a long holiday and look at it as something that one day I should find again – not realising how long that time would be.

Chapter Six

Three years passed, in some ways the happiest but in others the most destructive of my life. I had a lot to learn and absorb, and made a lot of new friends – but in the end had to admit that I had chosen the wrong profession. As for the destruction, it was literally a tragedy, life-stopping and incomprehensible.

I succeeded in getting into a new drama school run by Michel Saint-Denis, who had decided that England would give him a better chance of consolidating and putting into practice his new and fresh ideas. It was for Copeau that my father had done the clothes and scenery for *As You Like It* in the dim and distant past. I remember going to the audition with my mother, completely out of her depth in the world of the theatre, and shy, thinking no doubt of the way things looked, rather than of their literary distinction or the dramatic situation. As she and I sat in the darkened stalls, waiting for my turn, we became aware of a powerful presence, round which other people hummed like bees at a honey jar. This was Michel Saint-Denis, the director of the school and my future teacher, for whose paternal eye I immediately conceived a total respect.

In spite of the fact that he had never met her before, he greeted my mother with the special consideration usually reserved for old friends, while I, oddly not nervous, went on stage to perform the part of Millamant in *The Way of the World*. The part demanded, needless to say, a sophistication and a finesse of which I was incapable (it had been my brother Justin who'd recommended it to me); but, because of my mother, I was accepted – on probation – and went home with my heart full of excitement.

I was too unformed, too lacking in independence to realise it at the time, but it was unfortunate that, everywhere I went, I was illuminated by the spotlight of my parents' fame and reknown, although that in itself was nothing compared with that of others. Admittedly it was a privilege, but it was also a straitjacket from which I never succeeded in freeing myself. However much I wriggled, like a fish *en gelée*, I remained vague and insubstantial. I am sure that I had it in me to be an actress but, like other young people, I needed help – and at home I found none, or not of the kind I needed.

I was given the part of Irina in *Three Sisters*. It was my opportunity – a marvellous one. I looked perfect for it and should have had no difficulty in becoming this supremely innocent, fresh young girl. But something, like a ghastly sickness, prevented me. The part did not grow wings. I grew limp and unconvincing, and envied Olga and Masha their ability to catch on to reality. I now think that had I implored Saint-Denis for help, he would have given it to me. But either I was too ignorant or too proud – I don't know which it was, but he failed me (and now that I come to think of it he may have been too attracted to me, and was therefore paralysed). And I did not have the courage to ask him; it was after all his job to direct me, and mine only to do what I was directed to do. So he told me nothing. There was, between us, a block which only a much more mature woman could have broken down, and afterwards, although I said nothing, I felt a hidden resentment which I am only now, at least fifty years later, beginning to understand. At all events the part was taken from me and I well remember the moment at which Saint-Denis said, quite simply, that he had changed the cast – and how I had quickly hidden my feelings, pretending to be full of understanding. The part of Irina was given to a friend of mine, Yvonne Mitchell, a beautiful and intelligent girl who later, from sheer hard work, became a well-known actress. People were, of course, kind to me – but no one told me the truth, or insisted on my understanding it.

All this time, my brother Justin was feeling more and more isolated in China. He was, no doubt, right to have gone there, right to have taught the Chinese a few words of English, right to have tried to separate himself from his mother, for a time. If he had taught, he had also learned – and not least from the many love affairs he had

had – although he had never learned not to hurt people unnecessarily, particularly women. Fundamentally, it was a question of responsibility – and perhaps that would come later. Although China had become a real place to him, it remained on the other side of the world and out of reach. He had given it what he could – a gift that amazed and delighted the Chinese. But he did not speak the language, he was lonely; and events in Europe were rapidly changing. It was evident that an international war would soon break out. Things were becoming clearer, and with the clarity came the greenish light of the devil, and the certainty that one could only win by offering all one had. Justin had to be at home, on hand. He could not remain aloof on the other side of the world.

So, on a boat and enjoying himself still, back he came, his mind already made up. He imagined he could go direct to Spain where the war had already started – but of course such an idea, if put into practice, would have classified him as a monster of insensitivity. Had he for-gotten his mother, his dearest friend? Had he forgotten all his other friends and relations whom he had known all his life? He had to go back and face them, lined-up and bristling with counter-arguments to stop him going. If war was coming, he would do better to wait for the crunch, they said. But when they saw him – with his hair cut short and in his Chinese robes – they realised that their arguments did not stand a chance. He had crossed the invisible line between them and his own exaulted ideals. His mother was the only person he would listen to – she persuaded him to drive an ambulance rather than be a common soldier. This was, of course, the thing he wanted most of all: had he not written that the only thing he had missed in a very happy life was the experience of war? Nonetheless he gave in to her, and was allotted an ambulance by the English authorities.

He did not have to wait long for his orders. When the command came he was ready, at our family house so near the sea, to leave the past and confront the unknown future. But, ready though he was, he could not get the ambulance to start – it seemed like a jinx on the whole enterprise. In desperation he tinkered with the mechanics, and after an hour or two got the engine started. There was a last embrace with Mother – a feeling of warmth and beauty – and then she came home alone, while he crossed the Channel in a state of exhilaration. He was thrust into a position of responsibility as the only one who could speak French, and felt born again, with a new skin, and an inexhaustible amount of energy – also a new feeling of pride in himself. They entered Spain, and eventually he made it to the front and saw the war he had always imagined, and was both horrified and impressed by its brutality, combined with its devastating finality.

Together he and his friends made a coherent group of young men, prepared to risk everything for what they believed in. It was a challenge that Justin met with gaiety and courage, and in doing so impressed those around him. At first he was disappointed at not being in the centre of things, but after a month or two, when the great attack came and more men were needed, he was moved to the most dangerous area of all. There he worked long into the night carrying the wounded off the battle-ground, and there the battle was relentless, allowing few to escape. One day he was fatally wounded, and fell to the ground so covered with mud and dirt as to be unrecognisable. Eventually, washed and cleaned, he was laid out on the surgeon's table half-conscious, and as white as snow. The surgeon, an old friend, listened to his last words, which were confused and unintelligible, but happy. At last he knew what war meant – and he died without regaining consciousness.

I learned of his death in the middle of our end-of-term festivities, when my father and younger brother had appeared just in time to see me dance in a dramatic ballet, the plot of which was, absurdly enough, inspired by Goya's *Desastres de la Guerra*. I had to ask permission to leave and go home to my mother, in desperate need of support. I climbed the ladder to where Saint-Denis was sitting, watching and controlling the performance. I didn't need to say much – my condition spoke for itself – and he came down, took me in his arms, and gave me a comforting bear hug. The rest I do not remember – only how sweet this was in the midst of all the agony that followed, having nothing and yet everything to do with me. I had one intimate moment with my mother, in bed and distorted by grief. I said I had always known this would happen – and so, she said, had she. Then silence fell, and I was relegated to a no-man's-land, where my feelings, though strong, were unrecognised, so I appeared not to have any.

Chapter Seven

It was now that the real war was looming, like a disease that carried destruction within its bowels, threatening but, for the moment, painless. It was something we lived through, something we never would have chosen, only conceivable because we could do nothing else. We had to survive. So we closed our eyes and ears to the horrors, and thought only of victory, though at that time victory seemed nothing more than a faraway dream.

Aurore was born to Juliana and Gilles, and then grew, to take her first steps in a world that, though still sending up brilliant sparks of protest, was doomed to extinction. And when extinction came too close, all but singeing the wings of Gilles – whose blood was of the wrong colour – Aurore hid with her mother deep in the country, too young to know perhaps, but not too young to feel. Juliana stayed and protected her daughter as best she might, ignorant of Gilles's fate. Only one thing do I remember, that while out walking, she and Aurore met a lone man with a gun in a remote and scarcely trodden wood. Quite obviously he was on the lookout, and they beat a hasty retreat. Luckily it was their only contact with the Maquis.

And I in London, now married to a man much older than I was, experienced a different war. My husband was in the Intelligence Service and knew a great deal about what was happening; but he could not discuss it. Occasionally he would bring home with him someone who had been dropped by parachute into France, and who had come back to tell the story of his adventures – a story where of course everything was shrouded in secrecy. But I was surrounded by friends, unsuspecting of the kind of evil that faced us. Though we talked of the war and, in my family at least, it was the subject of a passionate daily argument, this evil washed over me and left me in ignorance. Like many people, I knew very little of the Holocaust or the concentration camps – indeed the true horror of their existence only became apparent at the very end of the war, when the appalling photographs were published in the papers. Some, perhaps many, would have called this egotistical but, as for most people, wisdom only came to me afterwards. And all this time my belly was growing larger and I was absorbed by the strange mystery of creation, of making a new life in the midst of all this destruction. My eldest daughter Nina was born and took every ounce of my energy. I had little thought for anyone else.

But my war also included the buzz bombs – those macabre engines we first saw flying through the night like a weapon conceived by Leonardo da Vinci. So bizarre were they that, watching from the roof, we hardly realised that this flaming monstrosity was dangerous until, at last, it exploded. It missed us by about a mile, leaving us shaken but whole. My husband Edward, who was too old to be called up, was wholeheartedly pro-war. His job meant that we had to live in London, and so learned to cope with the blackouts, rationing, air-raids, rockets and buzz bombs and queuing for the bare necessities of life. I did these things like everyone else, but war created a deep fear within me which it took me years to get over.

For me the blackout symbolised the snuffing out of culture: painting, music and joyous reunions were things you had to fight for. They became an underground activity, which nevertheless continued to exist, and were all the more prized for the energy they needed – I could not have survived without them. Yet I had little to complain about: I was protected by a loving husband, and my family still welcomed me for weekends in the rambling old house in the country where my mother – her face now furrowed like an old oak tree – continued bravely to plant vegetables, keep chickens and feed a pig, as well as painting still lifes and supporting the local art galleries. The life we had to lead was idiotic by all normal standards, but at the same time sadder and harder.

One evening as Edward and I were sitting at the supper table, the telephone rang. I went to answer it and heard over the wire a rather high-pitched voice, with a foreign accent. He asked for Mrs Thubron, my married name. I couldn't make out who it was. 'It's Gilles Deloiseau here. Do you remember me?' I was wildly excited and wanted him to come round at once. But he was in Kensington and the blackout was between us. We made a date for the following day and after we had rung off I went to tell my husband who it was. He was almost as excited as I was to meet someone just out of France.

When Gilles came to lunch he looked thin and tired though otherwise unchanged, except that he had shaved off his beard. He told us the story of his escape from France, which had not been without its perilous moments. He had spent some time in the Maquis – something that I found hard to imagine since Gilles was anything but an outdoor man. It had soon become unsafe, however, so he had gone to Algeria and from there managed to escape to England. He knew that Juliana and Aurore were somewhere in the Dordogne, but he had heard nothing directly from them and was very anxious. He found it a relief to tell us all this, and was affectionate, wanting to know about us and our life, and interested in my husband's work, which had changed, and now consisted of sending messages to the French Resistance and encouraging those who, over the now uncrossable Channel, were risking their lives in daily acts of courage. As for news of Aurore and Juliana, they could provide none.

But after the Battle of el Alamein in 1942, the war took a turning. Life lightened. People smiled a trifle more than before. Preoccupied with Nina, and then a second baby, providing food and simple, spiritual survival, I dreamed of life after the war, a return to the country, to a life that, incredibly enough, I took for granted, but which, it turned out, I would never know again.

In London, Gilles got a job with the Free French movement and was soon working as hard as ever. He was living in Kensington, in a place he thoroughly disliked, so, as we had taken a house in the country to be near my mother-in-law, we offered him our flat. He moved in before we left, and for a time we were all living together.

Without Juliana, Gilles was not only unhappy: he was lost. He was like a shorn sheep that has lost its tail as well. There was no one to find his socks or braces in the morning, or to tell him what to eat. He skimmed the only remnant of cream to be found on the milk and threw it down the drain because, he said, it gave him indigestion. We gave him a few meals, but often he would eat out and if he came in late would only munch a crust of bread and drink some cold coffee. He complained a lot about English food, and said that above all the coffee here was worse than in France. I reminded him that there was a war on and thought it odd that he should object to the second-rate, when he came from a country where, now at least, there was no coffee at all.

I can't remember for how long we all shared the same apartment, but in the end Gilles got on our nerves. When we went I left Mrs Purcell, our char as we called her, to look after him. She was a buxom but hideous woman with leering eyes that winked continuously as though she were drunk. She came every morning at nine on the dot, puffing and blowing up the staircase with some story that held the other lodgers up to ridicule. Needless to say she disapproved of Gilles simply because he was French. When I said he was being hunted by the Nazis, a brave man escaped from dire peril with a wife and child left in danger, she simply grunted and showed the whites of her eyes, hinting that he would soon find someone else in England. By and by she realised how useless he was and despised him more and more openly, secretly delighting in her contempt.

Grudgingly she would help him find the things he had lost, presenting him with his attaché case and a 'There you are, Mr Jill. It's surprising how you always find what's missing if you look for it.' Gilles was, of course, quite unaware of her meaning – and indeed of her general manner. He worried that so many things disappeared just when he needed them, and was grateful to her for finding them.

Gilles lived alone in the flat during the summer, seeing my husband when Edward needed to spend the night in London. Aware that my husband was, apart from his war job, a distinguished modern author, Gilles, reluctant to lose a golden moment, talked to him whenever possible of Shakespeare. He would take Edward to the Potomac restaurant in Jermyn Street, and give him exceedingly expensive sliced kidneys on toast with small pieces of tomato. The whole place was draped with stars and stripes and the menu was served by starched and servile waiters. In guiding the conversation to Shakespeare, Gilles would ask fundamental questions about *Othello* or *Hamlet*. Edward would give the best reply he could muster and then, after twenty minutes, would think of the reply he should have made. Gilles would listen to my husband – a very slow talker – for as long as he could bear to, then interrupt and show, by what he said, that he had misunderstood everything.

Chapter Eight

The summer went on. News from France was scarce and uncertain. Eventually Gilles heard from Juliana and, after an interval, she and Aurore managed to get to London and moved into our flat. Everything changed for Gilles. The centre had returned to his life.

Juliana was a sombre figure in London. She walked slowly through the bomb-stricken streets, plunged deep into her private thoughts with none of the life and spirit she had had in Paris. A little stouter, greyer and slower, she still wore the sweeping skirts and long black cape, while her hair lay flat and scraped back into a small bun to reveal her broad forehead and wide-apart, intelligent green eyes. And beside her now marched the small, stalwart figure of Aurore, who had the same long, curly mouth and the lively expression of someone so far undaunted, living intensely and often laughing. Now about six years old, she clung to Juliana, finding herself suddenly in a strange country with incomprehensible habits and an unknown language. But she was full of affection and immediately took to me, asking questions and making jokes. We did all sorts of things together, such as going to the zoo, where Aurore suddenly spat out of her mouth the monkey nuts she had been eating, thinking they had been contaminated by a small chimpanzee who had put his arm out of the cage to ask for more. Juliana did not come with us. She was exhausted by living in the French countryside, where she had not had enough to eat, and had been forced to stay with people she neither liked nor trusted.

Eventually Juliana and Gilles found a little house behind Harrods that looked fine from the outside but was very depressing within. It was furnished with red plush curtains and mahogany furniture and was dark and poky. Although they put a good face on it, the whole family seemed out of place. Aurore was miserable in her school, where they obviously thought she was badly brought up. Gilles was overworked, and Juliana in a state of mind bordering on suicidal depression.

Eventually we went down to the country and they moved into our flat. I had left strict orders with Mrs Purcell to go there every morning, but after some time I discovered that she hardly ever turned up. Enquiry elicited the information that she had left for good as she had found a better job elsewhere. By that time she truly loathed Mr Jill – and Mrs Jill was there to do the work herself.

I would have given a lot to help Juliana had I seen more of her. She was too depressed to start painting and hardly read a book. When I went to London I found her exhausted after cooking supper, waiting for Gilles to come in. She was always affectionate to me, but not communicative. She told me afterwards that, having come near to committing suicide, she was only saved by an honest doctor, who gave her a tiny homeopathic pill and said, 'This will either kill or save you – take it and good luck!' Juliana took it and got better, though there was a rumour that, while Juliana and Aurore were hiding in the depths of the French countryside, Gilles had fallen, as Mrs Purcell suggested, for someone else. What kind of woman had attracted him and who it was, I never knew. In view of his evident devotion to Juliana it did not seem to matter much. But Juliana, romantic, single-minded and passionate, thought otherwise and her manner became, on occasion, almost icy. In any case it was evident that the relationship with Gilles was no longer the most important thing in her life; Aurore was now the one who counted.

The war was coming to an end. Paris was liberated so Juliana and Aurore went back to pick up the threads of their previous life in a shattered and stunned France. Whilst Gilles was left in London to round off his work before joining them. He moved back into the flat, and we were also there at that time and lived with him while anticipating his departure. The news came at last that he was to take an aeroplane at seven in the morning. The evening before we said goodbye with much affection and goodwill and went to bed. Gilles stayed up, packing. He paced up and down the room above our heads. Occasionally we heard the door shut – he was going into another room. Surely now he will go to bed, we thought, lying below, sleepless. No! Back he came, the never-ending footsteps sounding again above our heads. At two in the morning we finally dropped off . . . At five there was a disturbance. We awoke. Of course, Gilles had to catch his plane. We listened. After a long time during which we heard him packing now in earnest, there was a ring at the bell. He went down, and then came up again to fetch his bag. At last he went down and we heard the front door slam. We sighed and turned over, hoping for sleep. But no! He was back again – and this time my husband had to go down and open the front door – having forgotten the most important thing of all, the little case with his papers in it. This time he went, not to return – back to France, Paris, Auteuil, his apartment and French family life . . .

Four years passed. My two girls kept me constantly occupied, and I had no time to go over to Paris. I kept in touch with Juliana and Gilles mostly by letter. I heard how Aurore got on at school and how they had bought a house in the country. It was to this house, in the peaceful land of the Oise, that I took the children and went to stay with them.

It was a large house built in the shape of an L, with one side facing the village street. This was the side we occupied; it was the oldest part of the house with pretty, eighteenth-century rooms and a big, old kitchen. Juliana occupied the other wing which was new and stretched into the garden. There was a large studio on the first floor and numerous bedrooms and an attic filled with junk. The park, as Juliana called it, was chiefly grass – yellow and dry owing to the hot summer. A goat or two rattled their chains and munched anything they could get. Beyond this was a vegetable garden, with rows of excellent pear trees. The village was inescapable on one side, with its *épicerie*, butcher's shop and *mairie*, but in the garden, immersed in our own affairs, we were unaware of it, and could only hear and smell the farm next door where we collected our milk each day.

Juliana was more like she had been before the war. The spaciousness of the house and garden suited her. She was completely at home, gathering in her harvest of pears or going for country walks in her low-heeled velvet slippers. She enjoyed being in the country to the full and having the choice of such large rooms, with a sizeable studio really worthy of the name.

Yet she said she was tired and wanted only peace and quiet – and was not sure if she could do any work. We were only the first to invade this charmed peace and very soon others arrived: Madame Héloïse Magnan with her little boy of eight or nine, and Aurore's music teacher, a lady with dark red hair, who also brought her little boy. I sometimes joined them for a meal or an after-dinner coffee, once my children were in bed, and the hubbub was tremendous. Both little boys were called François; both were brown-skinned, nice, intelligent and talkative. Their parents constantly corrected their behaviour, but the boys always answered back, so there was a double conversation continually going on: the grown-ups talking passionately about how to cook mackerel or what underclothes one should wear at the seaside, or whether Fauré could be compared with Mozart. And then the children would often ask questions while the mother said: 'Come here, François, you must pull up those pants, you can't go around looking like a chimpanzee', or 'Stop biting your nails, François. You will spoil your hands.'

Sometimes, for the sake of peace, the children were put to eat in another room, but this hardly improved matters – the grown-ups' talk was free to flow uninterrupted for the space of ten minutes and then suddenly there would be shrieks and howls, and one of the little boys would rush into the room, fling himself against his mother or stand in the middle of the doorway so that all eyes were fastened on him and yell: 'It's François, Maman. He emptied his glass of water on to my plate. I can't eat any more.' Or: 'It's François, Maman, he blew his nose over my food.' Severe reproofs followed these outbursts but the boys only returned to their places after each small victory over their mothers, with constant concessions having to be made.

Juliana would sit through these scenes without comment, eating her pear and quietly observing. If ever she asked one of the boys to do something for her they usually obeyed at once. Aurore would look on with a stare only to be described as enigmatic. Sometimes she rolled her eyes and exploded with laughter, or commented on this behaviour in asides to me, but I was always aware of the difference between her and these other children – a difference she was quite aware of herself. She was of course several years older than they were, and perhaps this explained it.

Madame Magnan was dark and ugly, but with the irrepressible vitality of the Midi. Words poured out of her mouth, rrrs were rolled with enthusiasm, and with hardly a pause for breath she would talk for hours. All the time she would also be cutting bread, clearing the table, looking at a magazine, or painting a picture. Interminable activity and expenditure of energy. I liked her – she was friendly and honest, and although she allowed them so little time to sink in, she was alive to new impressions.

As for Madame Steibert, she was really appalling, although it took Juliana some time to realise her limitations. More self-controlled than Madame Magnan, she chose those moments in which to speak when she could relate an anecdote on the best French style and everyone was obliged to listen. Her voice, clear, cool and rather high-pitched, would ring with just the right inflections and pauses as though the story had been rehearsed beforehand. The word '*spirituel*' was always on her lips and such expressions as '*d'une manière très fine*', or '*il jouait ça comme un ange, absolument comme un ange.*' She came from a different world and found it very difficult to adjust herself to Juliana's standards. Needless to say she was there because Juliana had taken pity on her. She was hard up and couldn't afford a holiday in a hotel. Juliana's cook – recently acquired – also came down with her tiny grandchild to spend some weeks in the country. This child was white and spotty, dressed in quilted clothes even during that terribly hot summer. He stayed up until eight or nine at night, and would then he carried to the top of the steps and made to wave his arm and say '*Bonsoir*' to everyone as many times as possible. This caused Juliana agony every evening. She would turn away her head and, with a bare wave of her hand, say in English: 'That's enough, that's enough! Do take that poor child away!'

Whether they were aware of it or not the birth of Aurore had cemented the lives of Juliana and Gilles more firmly together, and the upheaval of the war, which had shaken the whole of Europe, not to say the world, had taught them who they could rely on and who not. Although his little newspaper had not survived, Gilles had learned how few of his friends could really be trusted, and behaved with greater circumspection. He still worked hard at the Cour des comptes and only came down to the country at weekends. Juliana became a little slower and shabbier, wandering about in her velvet slippers and white stockings, her hair with threads of grey hanging down her back. She picked the fruit, learned to prune the trees and grew vegetables. But it was Aurore, growing up fast and full of gaiety, who was the kernel of their lives.

She was young – and very grown-up for her age. Her behaviour was not obviously spoiled, and there was no reason it should have been, and yet she was allowed to do all she wanted, and was treated like an adult. Among all these hangers-on Aurore moved like a princess, free but preoccupied with a secret and so far unannounced ambition. She was easy to live with and did what she was asked with gaiety and good humour. It was obvious she would not be a beauty, but there was something marvellously alive in her expression, and charming in her responses. She passionately adored her mother and was more critical towards her father, but was only completely happy when they were both there.

Towards my children she was the ideal older friend – amused, patient and kind. She was always ready to take them out for a walk, and when they were bored she would invent some game to amuse them. My elder child, Nina, might make a sculpture with her approval, and the younger one just enjoyed nestling up to her no matter what they did. At the same time Aurore did not allow herself to be monopolised. When she wanted to be alone she just disappeared.

Yet it was in the evenings that both Juliana and Aurore seemed to be possessed of some kind of extra energy, an electric current that passed from one to the other and often kept them in fits of laughter. We would all go to bed, and I would hear them through the open window in the other wing of the house, both in the same bed, roaring and shrieking with laughter. It was obvious they were enjoying themselves and that their relationship was both happy and joyously intimate. It was enough in itself and they needed no one else's company. I envied them their intimacy and the warmth that bound them together, so unlike my relationship with my own mother, on

Aurore's side so much more adult, and on Juliana's so much freer and more sympathetic.

After a time Gilles would appear from Paris, tired but gay, and delighted to pose as a lover of the country and walk round the park admiring the dessicated box bushes. With him he brought a brand-new Citroën car and a chauffeur.

There had been some talk about this car before his visit and Juliana was full of foreboding on the subject. She was convinced that Gilles would be unsafe on the road, and said that she herself had had forty lessons in driving, and still felt incapable of mastering the art which, she insisted, belonged to men more than women.

The car was black and shining. The chauffeur Gilles had brought with him from Paris got into it on the right and Gilles on the left, and everyone stood around to watch. As an experienced driver I was made to sit in the back seat while Gilles looked carefully at all the controls. 'This is the key to turn on the engine,' he said, turning it on, 'this is the self-starter', pressing it, 'now I let off the brake, de-clutch, put it into first, let the clutch in – and she starts.' To my surprise, after these lengthy proceedings, she did start. Slowly we went round the village, and except for the fact that he couldn't slow the car down at the blind corners – of which there were plenty – he didn't do badly at all. When we got on to the main road all went swimmingly, although he was terrified by cyclists and pedestrians. It took him at least half a mile to decide where to turn round, but he finally managed it and we returned to the village. I was quite impressed by his efficiency and hurried to tell Juliana and Aurore all about it. Juliana had by now dressed herself in black satin shoes with small heels and was prepared to take her turn. She was very deliberate and stately, obviously doing what she considered to be her duty yet against her will. She sighed with the effort and sat down in the car. 'Oh, Agnès, I shall never be a driver you know. It's beyond me at my age.' Actually more sure of herself than Gilles had been, she went through the same preliminary magic. The car started with a roar. Juliana was delighted. 'Ah! *Tu vois!* It's not so bad. Off we go.' We skimmed round the first corner and round the second and third; the idea that there might be an old horse and cart round the bend never seemed to cross her mind for an instant. Out on the high road with great aplomb we went, passing others with perfect assurance. We came to a town. 'Ah! Agnès, I can't turn round – I shall go back this way.' So we avoided having to turn the car and came home in triumph.

From this moment the car became a part of our lives, but Juliana seldom, if ever, drove it. It was Gilles who took it to Paris, looked after it, and cared about it. But in the end he realised that it was more trouble than it was worth, and the car was forgotten.

Chapter Nine

It must have been the following year that Aurore came to spend the summer holidays with us in England. Though only fifteen she behaved as a mature adult, at least on the surface. She and Nina were inseparable. Friends came to stay, we went on all sorts of outings and enjoyed ourselves. Aurore had little difficulty with English, the reason being, quite simply, that she wanted to learn. The only thing for which she seemed ungifted was the piano. She spent many hours sitting in front of it, but showed little improvement, something that might be put down to the appallingly conventional French teaching. It may also have been too inhibiting to have Madame Eckhardt in the background. Hearing the little sonata by Mozart she had chosen to learn, played again and again in the sitting room, always with the same mistakes, I would put my head in at the door to see her unruly head of dark hair bent and shaken over the piano keys in desperation, since what she wanted was perfection – an impossible desire.

One morning Aurore came down to breakfast saying that the picture hanging over her bed had fallen in the night and hit her on the head. But she was young and elastic and I was not particularly worried; however, Aurore

155

wrote to Juliana about it, who of course telephoned to find out exactly what had happened and the whole incident became a drama. From this moment on Aurore started to sulk. She became restless, and it was clear that our family life bored and irritated her. She had very beautiful grey-blue eyes with dark lashes, and when friends came to tea she would sit and stare at them in a disconcerting and infuriating way, evidently hoping to make an impression, an aim in which she was not disappointed. One of them even complained to me of 'your young friend – she stares at me enough to be embarrassing.' I mentioned this to Aurore but without much effect, and slowly found myself slipping into the role of one who is hypnotised, the follower rather than the mature leader. Aurore had quite as much charisma or force of personality as Juliana, and would no doubt rule over another, just as Juliana did over Gilles. She had a very exalted idea of herself and her gifts, and no one could deny her intelligence. Had she not been of a sweet disposition with great generosity, she might well have been intolerable. But seeing how she vibrated with life and enjoyment, all criticism appeared meaningless. She missed Juliana and, after the first interest and excitement of being in a foreign country with a family she was fond of, she longed for her home – so different from ours, I now see, with its atmosphere of warmth and affection.

The experience of staying with us had helped to mature her however. On her return to Paris she persuaded Gilles and Juliana, both sticklers for education, to allow her to leave school ahead of time, with the idea that she should take her Bachot – the equivalent of the School Certificate of those days – at any time she wished. She was dying to go on the stage, to become an actress – and indeed seemed to have the temperament required. She reminded me of Henry James's *The Tragic Muse*, coming as she did from a family entirely unconnected with the theatre.

It was a relief when Aurore finally returned to Paris. The few weeks spent in England were of course labelled a success, but I was well aware that Aurore was glad to go. And this was perhaps natural, although it was true that there had been something ill-adapted and puzzling in her behaviour – a behaviour that could not be blamed on me and which I myself was probably too inexperienced to understand.

Had I been as truly honest as I intended to be, I might have seen that I had been trying to play a role I was not really suited for. Caught between Juliana and Aurore, I had, for no reason at all – or rather because I regarded Juliana as an absolute authority whose influence had been paramount in my own life – actually tried to adopt this same authority in relation to Aurore. I had tried, in good faith, to be a substitute mother – and of course was not up to it. For if anyone resembled Juliana, it was certainly not me. I was too young, too shallow and in many ways too conventional. Juliana, in her perfectly natural although somewhat exaggerated anxiety at parting for the first time from her beloved daughter, had to a certain extent brainwashed me into believing that I had a responsibility for Aurore, when in fact I had very little. And Aurore herself, more enlightened and sensitive than me, and with all the pride and vitality of extreme youth, had enjoyed her own ability to dominate and to subjugate the feebler me, by an emotional power that was a part of her gift as an actress.

The next time I went to Paris, fairly soon afterwards, Aurore would recite speeches to me from Corneille or Racine and I realised that, although at present she lacked any experience, she had a remarkable talent. Still she seemed at the mercy of her own emotions. Something, somewhere, was causing her trouble. For one thing, she would not eat, and when she did, would show every sign of feeling sick. Her thick, curly hair started to come out. When she brushed or combed it she left whole wads of it on her clothes or on the floor. And as she grew taller and more womanly in shape, with a well-formed bust and shoulders, she also grew thinner. She now dressed with panache, albeit with a style reminiscent of Juliana – long cloaks, with small high-heeled slippers and pale-coloured stockings. She saw herself as an attractive and dynamic woman, born of a very remarkable and rather intimidating mother, and such was the truth; yet she was still the child, the young and spoiled daughter, who would have to make an effort to free herself from such an influence. She could not exist without Juliana. Their relationship was still symbiotic and passionate – one was a reflection of the other, and Gilles was the stage-struck, but also concerned, observer.

One evening I happened to drop round at their apartment and found Aurore alone, with only old Madame Eckhardt there as a kind of *chien de garde*. Gilles, summoned by his employers, had taken Juliana with him on a short journey to Scandinavia, leaving their daughter to the care of her grandmother. They were to go by air, and I found Aurore *dans tous ses états*, waiting for the promised message of their safe arrival. It was about nine in the evening, and still no message had been received. 'Oh! Agnès, my darling, come and help me wait. I can't go to bed without knowing they've arrived. Come and talk to me or, rather, I will recite something I have just learned – an English poem.' And, standing in the middle of the room, with a face of anxious ecstasy, she began to recite Elizabeth Barrett Browning, rather as Gilles might have done:

And, as I mused it in his antique tongue,
I saw, in gradual vision through my tears,

The sweet, sad years, the melancholy years,
Those of my own life, who by turns had flung
A shadow across me. Straightway I was 'ware,
So weeping, how a mystic Shape did move
Behind me, and drew me backward by the hair;
And a voice said in mastery, while I strove –
'Guess now who holds thee?' –
'Death,' I said. But, there,
The silver answer rang, – 'Not Death, but Love.'

And Aurore sank into a chair, as though momentarily defeated after a triumph.

Aurore, who never did anything in quite the same way as anyone else, did go to an acting school, where there were classes of only ten or fifteen pupils. She soon became the favourite pupil of her teacher, the then famous actress Maria Casares. At nineteen or twenty, although, as we know, she could not be called beautiful, she had a youthful presence and dignity together with a vibrant vitality that was very appealing. She was capable of thinking for herself, ready to account for her feelings and the nascent splendour of her vision of life. Neither was she deficient in a sense of humour, frequently laughing and teasing her companions with a *sans-gêne* they appreciated for its affection and spontaneity. Few of them equalled her in sensitivity or a sort of superior consciousness of the role that she wanted to play in life. There was no doubt she expected to be at the forefront of things, and took it for granted that such was her rightful place.

Maybe Aurore was in love. But with whom, and why it turned out to be an unhappy experience, I did not know. Juliana told me a little – but was extremely discreet, keen on playing down the whole thing and avoiding dramatising an experience that might have meant the end of Aurore's ambitions as an actress. But I did hear more about it from Aurore herself one evening when we were out walking in the Luxembourg Gardens. 'Darling Agnès, I don't know what Juliana has told you, but someone very important has come into my life, and I want to ask your advice. I am in love.' I didn't know why she spoke in English. Perhaps it all sounded further away, less immediate. 'And it is wonderful because we are both interested in the same things. He goes to the same classes I do – he is gifted – but he is older and we see a lot of each other. He and I are in a play about Don Giovanni – I am Donna Anna, and have been told that I am very good.' She stopped to shake her head and say, 'But not so good I couldn't be better. I have just been told' – and here Aurore tried hard not to cry – 'he is married and, I believe, has a child. What am I to do? I must give him up – but how can I?'

I listened, and was worried. What indeed could she

do? 'Aurore,' I said, wanting to know more, 'how much have you seen him – how much have you had to do with him?'

'I have seen him several times outside classes. We met in a café, and I fell in love at once. Or, at least that is not true. I was already pretty far gone, since seeing him in the part of Hippolytus – but I cannot stop thinking of him.'

I looked at her, and saw how much thinner she had become, how there were shadows under her eyes, and how white her cheeks were. I felt like a murderer. 'You must banish him from your heart. He is not meant for you. If he has a child you would be doing a dreadful thing in tempting him away from his family. But perhaps it's more his responsibility to control himself and to leave you alone. Do you think he loves you?'

'I did think he was attracted – but I know you are right, and I must stop feeling like this.' She was heroic, but unconvincing.

They saw each other whenever they rehearsed, and the situation in the play was exactly like what they might have wished it to be in real life – that is to say, it was passionate and committed, and essentially tragic. The young man, Paul I think he was called, was reasonably good-looking, but not very articulate, whereas Aurore found it much easier to say what she felt. This quality only made him less like Gilles, and therefore in her eyes more attractive. Nevertheless he was very attentive and bowled over by Aurore's vitality. She was freed from the ties that bound her, and it was this, I suppose, that seemed to her so marvellous. She had hoped for a permanent relationship, but now of course it was out of the question. She needed help, but there was no one but me whom she could ask – and I could only say what was obvious.

One of her teachers told her that she was a very interesting actress, the best Donna Anna he'd yet had. 'You are very good,' he said and told her she had the dignity and sweetness of the Spaniard. 'I will work on this scene with you so as to improve it. You must make the audience believe that she is going to die, she suffers so much.' Aurore was delighted, but protested that she probably ought to have waited until the last sentence to reveal all the violence. 'It doesn't matter,' he replied, 'there are many interesting qualities in what you do,' and there was no doubt he saved her from a deep depression by his praise. She longed to put on armour and fight for what she believed in – and it was perhaps this conviction that was necessary for success. And although I had given up the stage, I still clung to the idea of 'what might have been'; my giving up had been a sham, and I was intent on making this ravishing and innocent creature pay for my failure.

It was probably about now that I took it into my head,

for no reason at all, to write Juliana a letter. The impulse arose, justifiable as I thought then, from my effort to play the role of substitute mother – a role that, in view of Juliana's own existence, was obviously redundant. Abysmally ignorant of my own motivations and unwilling to recognise the cowardice from which they arose, I criticised Aurore (nicely of course) for those aspects of behaviour in which she was so very much my superior: her uncompromising honesty and straightforwardness, her luminous courage. I clothed these sentiments in language that obscured my true intentions – which, of course, I did not myself recognise – and which Juliana accepted at their face value. Having sent it I was seized with tell-tale apprehension, anxious as to what Juliana would say. But I need not have worried. Juliana accepted my version of Aurore's behaviour as the mature and even helpful opinion of an old friend. True, Juliana had always given me credit for being more intelligent and mature than I was. This was due in part to her assumption that everyone was worthy of at least some respect, and partly a feeling that any member of my family was bound to be honourable.

My relief at Juliana's reception of the letter was profound. Her answer practically said she agreed with me. She was quite unsuspicious of my motivations – so much so that I rose to the surface like a bubble, and then continued as usual. But this was deceptive – in reality I could not forget what I had done, and hid behind Juliana's lack of understanding. Nevertheless, she must have said something that aroused Aurore's suspicion of my good faith. The next time I went to Paris I was not surprised to find that Aurore's greeting was chilly. She took her distance and remained there, saying all the usual things, but without the customary warmth – and with a look in her grey eyes that made me feel like a traitor and struck at my guilty conscience. Whatever it was that had pushed me to write the letter, it was poisoned – I was caught in a trap and could not escape. Had I then said, 'Aurore, darling, forgive me,' all would have been well. I would have found an explanation that she would have accepted and, after some reproaches and a few tears, we would have made it up and could have been closer than before. I might even have been more honest with myself. But something prevented me from any such transparence. I longed for grace, but my ego demanded recognition and I remained silent, giving myself the air of the victim, the one who needs an apology – and Aurore seemed as paralysed as I was. The expression in her eyes lay between us like the sword of Damocles. Going out together, as we continued to do, we would end up sitting in a café with nothing to say to each other. Had I been able to wrest it from its stagnant position I might have become mistress of my own life but, so profoundly incapable was I of putting myself in her place or thinking objectively, I could not shake off this devil.

Even before slipping the letter into the pillar box I had known that Juliana shared her correspondence with Aurore. Had I not heard late at night in the country, when Aurore slipped into Juliana's bed, their peals of laughter over letters received from Madame Eckhardt or other friends? Aurore boasted that she was her mother's confidante – trustworthy and intimate to a degree that I envied, never having had that sort of relationship with my own mother. There was no doubt that I knew that Aurore would read the letter, and come to her own conclusions. And in that letter I had shown myself as a traitor, uncaring and insensitive, offering a friendship with one hand which I took away with the other. As one of her closest friends, I had written not to her but to her mother, treating Aurore as though she did not exist. She had of course primarily relied on Juliana, but Juliana had for some reason failed her – why Aurore did not know, and Juliana did not explain. She had no need to, and Aurore, in the generosity of her heart, did not press her. She was perhaps too deeply wounded and now could not turn to Juliana or me. So, I was forced to ask myself, what had been my intention in writing it?

Was I still suffering from my failure to be an actress,

the missed opportunity of leading other people's lives – or had I never been intended for the theatre, which I undoubtedly saw in all its glamour rather than in its more serious aspects? For me, it was only an opportunity to shine and, in shining, to outshine everyone else. But my shining had always been dim and had never had the originality, or the gift that might have been expected of it and above all I lacked the honesty to admit this.

And into the bargain Aurore was Juliana's most precious possession. This, of course, was so right and so natural that it did not occur to me that I was jealous. A formidable legacy of oughts and shoulds obscured the shameful workings of my heart. If at times I suspected that I was guilty of feelings I could not acknowledge I hastily scraped up the dirt to hide a truth I could not face. Moreover, whenever possible I continued to trade on Juliana's generosity, not only receiving, but expecting, the warm welcome that Juliana always gave me. I was treated as a member of the family and, whenever I found myself in Paris, was expected to drop in for a casual meal or accompany them to the cinema or to the theatre, or simply take a bus down to St-Germain with them and sit in a café, watching the crowds – the smart women and the attractive men, sipping their drinks and smoking their cigarettes.

I had an Italian friend who lived in the rue St-André-des-Arts, to whom I introduced Aurore, hoping they would become friends, and that such an event would widen Aurore's horizon. This friend, Gina, younger than me, was infinitely more experienced and mature. She had a warmth of temperament that equalled Juliana's, and was at a moment in her life when, happily in love, she was at the centre of a small group of people who both prized and relied on her, seeing in her a vitality that they themselves lacked, but that she, like Juliana, could give off endlessly. I remembered one occasion, sitting on the pavement on a hot summer's afternoon with Gina and Aurore, still at the stage of shy politeness with each other – they were probably discussing some book or film recently seen or read – when Aurore said something rash, innocent and personal to which I replied with an unexpected brutality that made her turn white. She remained silent, evidently hurt and surprised – perhaps above all that her *chère* Agnès could so suddenly prove cruelly unkind. Gina covered the awkward moment while I, conscious of having committed a gross, nearly unforgivable fault, continued to smile and gossip as though nothing had happened. Later I felt so ashamed, so much so that I could never remember exactly what it was I had said, nor judge whether, had I confessed the complexity of my feelings to Aurore, forgiveness would have been forthcoming – or indeed whether it would have been justified. It was an occasion when, astonished at myself, I felt as though the remark had been made by someone else, a little devil sitting on my shoulder intent on betraying my real state of mind – the depths of treachery and jealousy from which I was actually suffering.

It is quite likely that Aurore's problems originated with an attempt to emancipate herself from her relationship with her mother as much as anything else. Juliana was over-anxious and, in spite of all her admirable qualities, had bred in Aurore an anguished reaction. As a result, Aurore had had to bear her own anxiety at growing up as well as the possessive fussing – for even Juliana could not escape this – and the all too attentive observation of both Juliana and Gilles who, passive as I may have made him appear, was as romantically in love with his daughter as was healthy and natural.

When I went to Paris I nearly always took with me a present for Aurore. Once it had been a complete annotated and illustrated edition of Jane Austen. The year after, having totally forgotten this, and searching desperately at the last minute for something to take, I chose the same again, albeit in a different edition. When Aurore saw this she received it with her customary directness. 'But, Agnès darling, you have already given me this! Don't you remember?' And her voice unconsciously carried with it the reproach implied by such forgetfulness. Had I forgotten my devoted and affectionate friend? Forgotten, that is, her specialness, her inner core, the fact that she was Aurore Deloiseau and no one else? I no doubt frowned, and was silent. I brushed it off, but always remembered it.

I did not 'mean' to hurt Aurore – or so I thought; that is to say, I did not think at all. What did I mean? Who did I think I was? What had I to do with innocence, or innocence with me? It was a mere smokescreen. It was only another word for criminality, and I was, without realising it, within an ace of committing such a crime – indeed I had committed it, and found myself with the reflection of my own ugliness. For what was the difference between me who, with one cruel and insensitive word, could hurt a loving and generous young creature – and a monster?

Although seventeen years older than Aurore, I had not learned to be humble, nor had time made me any wiser. There was in me a hard core of resistance which, had I realised it, had nothing to do with Aurore, and everything to do with myself and my lack of self-knowledge. In the deepest recesses of my nature I was deeply ashamed, but the worse I felt, the more difficult it became to confess – and as I never did so, I could not be forgiven. Thus I was not only the criminal but the judge – a judge deprived of the opportunity to be merciful and, not having the courage to confess my crime, I pretended I had not committed it. As a result I found myself plunged up to my ears in the slough of despond. If Aurore was the victim of my incomprehensible behaviour, she was at least innocent, and if she suffered from something, she did not understand what it might be. Though still a student, Aurore at least had the satisfaction of being a success, whereas I stood alone on an unknown shore, paralysed and guilty.

Nevertheless I had one more chance. Irina I could never be, nor have any success of that kind. Enthusiastic crowds and the heady excitement I had once dreamed of were not for me. Success had been important – but it was now out of reach. Instead I saw my behaviour for what it was: 'jealousy'. If I did not, as Juliana did, believe in God, I certainly believed in fate. My gods were the Greek gods, implacable and unforgiving, and they understood to what lengths innocence can be mistaken for its opposite, and how one can be blinded by a speck of dust that lodges in the eye and swells to enormous proportions.

I had committed a crime which, apparently, went unnoticed. It seems to me impossible that Juliana, on receiving my letter, should not have been at least mildly shocked by the contents and, but for some accident, would probably not have shown it to Aurore. Afterwards

I know that she threw it away; no proof remained therefore of what some would have called my true nature. Juliana's loyalty saved me, though – one can never tell – it might have been better for us all had she put the cards on the table. If she saved me from making an impossible explanation, she condemned me, given my cowardice, to a guilty silence, and her daughter to the frustration of being unable either to defend herself or to accuse me.

I ask myself, am I making a mountain out of a molehill? But if so, haven't I failed to see the point? However large or small, molehills are always molehills. It's not their size that matters, but their quality. It's what they are made of that betrays them. Dig into mine, for example, and you would find a desert, parched and dry, incapable of the generosity that Juliana had shown to me. My only sign of grace was my consciousness of guilt – but a feeling of guilt does not get one anywhere, it merely inhibits. If it points the way, it is through an undergrowth so thick and thorny that once in it you are lost.

Perhaps my worst fault was that I forgot to think of Aurore as a live young woman with a life of her own. Coming from my background, it was all the worse that I should have so little idea of the insensitivity of my behaviour – and the result was like the slamming of an iron door. For Gilles and Juliana it was a tragedy, but for me it was a sign, something I was meant to read, and later understand.

I lived this story, as I began to tell it, a long time ago, when I was young and skinless. It was Juliana and Gilles that I fell in love with, and of whose generosity I took advantage. If I fell in love with Aurore it was – and this I only understood years later – of a different kind. It was a brew mixed by the devil, green in colour and bitter to taste. Aurore was not only charming, desirable and intelligent, she was supremely gifted, thus putting my own talents in the shade. Where I failed she had succeeded, and was marked out by life as someone to be seen and remembered.

I was the older, and should have been the more mature. But I had not yet learned to be responsible. I had no idea, or only the dimmest one, of how intelligent and sensitive Aurore was, and later, when it came to writing it down, I thought I could play on the surface and tell it quickly, and that to confess my fault would be all that was required of me. But this was a delusion. The story became alive. It had always been a part of my life but, as I now saw, not as the delightful, if sad, memory it should have been, but as a shadow large and dark, trembling over my head. It was no longer a story that, with luck, might make you cry – it had become an incubus full of poison that I could not shake off.

Chapter Ten

Aurore had an Achilles' heel. She was enormously ambitious, given that she bore the brunt, like me, of the concentrated adoration of her parents. True, they had been saner and more humanely, naturally loving parents than mine; but they too were artists, given to dreaming of the 'great', as were my parents – figures whom they worshipped from afar, with a certain feeling that somewhere and somehow there was a kinship between them. And yet, I could remember Juliana saying, 'You know, *ma chère petite Agnès*, I could not care less whether Aurore becomes a great actress or not. All I want is for her to have a good husband and lots of children.' And perhaps this was so. Juliana herself was so down to earth and, although temperamental, so aware of other people's needs that she erred, if at all, on the side of austerity, and certainly of modesty. And she saw ultimate success in such a publicly orientated profession as the theatre as a form of selling one's soul to the devil.

And so, when Aurore started complaining of the shape of her nose – which perhaps showed more affinity with Gilles's family than Juliana's – Juliana, despite an obscure feeling that this was a matter of extreme importance, dismissed the whole subject. For her, Aurore's nose was a part of Aurore, the child who had been a part of her, and as such was sacred. Why should she not accept that her nose was large and splendid, evidence of a strength of character that could not be denied? True, there had recently been rumours and examples of successful face-lifting operations, where rich society women had their profiles altered to suit their ideals. They probably wanted to look like the idols of the American cinema – those unreal and atrocious beauties to whom such tortures seemed a necessary part of a life lived, according to Juliana, wrongly, and for the wrong reasons. A clinic full of impeccable white-clad nurses with painted faces, and doctors and specialists with horn-rimmed spectacles and beards, leaning solicitously over their beds, was also a kind of vision, a world of negative perfectionism which Juliana found perfectly horrifying.

It seemed an extraordinarily radical, not to say impertinent idea to change something that was so evidently an intimate part of you. Yet was it simply a question of temperament, the fact that Aurore, vibrating with a passionate ambition and, moreover, because so young, deeply unsure of herself, felt things more keenly and believed, for reasons that were totally obscure, that by changing her nose she could change herself? Edward, for one, told me of a woman he'd known who had done exactly the same thing and, instead of remaining her fascinating self, had become an uninteresting nonentity.

Was it a gesture of rejection, a semaphore message addressed to Juliana and Gilles saying, I love you but I've had enough of you. I want to live differently, to fly off on my own and be unrecognisable and ordinary, launching myself into a world of ordinary people who all have straight noses. Then I would be free, if I wanted, to go to Hollywood like Greta Garbo. Whereas, if I accept my nose as it is, I am condemned to the backwaters of the city and to the theatre of Cocteau, the Comédie Française, and all the intellectual Parisians.

Juliana may have understood something of all this. She may even have argued with Aurore. But these arguments, coming from such a source, inevitably fell on deaf ears. The more she and Gilles argued, the more Aurore clung to her idea. The more too her hair fell out, and the less she ate. As time went on, not wanting to talk any more about something that had become sore and painful, like a rotten tooth, she seemed to become privately obsessed, growing thinner and thinner and, though still apparently docile and affectionate, so clearly, if secretly unhappy, that for Juliana and Gilles life, instead of pursuing a delightful if headstrong course towards the future, turned and showed its other, darker side. Brought closer together not only by their deep disagreement with their daughter, but also by the paralysis her attitude had induced in them, Juliana and Gilles realised that their relationship – so far limpid and transparent – suddenly revealed itself as clouded and obscure.

Through all this Juliana knew very well that it is a law of nature for the child to disengage itself from its parents, and that the role of the parent is to stay solidly behind and watch attentively from a distance. And she and Gilles, trying to see the situation from the purely clinical, practical point of view, trying not to fuss nor make a fraught situation still more agonising, did indeed remind me of two birds sitting on the edge of a cliff, waiting for Aurore to spread her wings and launch herself into a space so high and so deep that, disappearing to a tiny spot in the distance, she would be divorced from all that had gone before. That would be the best that could happen since, although there was no real reason for their anxiety, there was always the possibility that her wings might fail her, and she would plunge into the abyss.

In English one says that you cut off your nose to spite your face. It is what people do when their pride has been deeply hurt. At the time of course no one thought of such a thing. Everyone's attention was concentrated on the physical and what one might call the moral, as opposed to the psychological aspect of the situation. And one of the questions in everyone's mind was: would the end justify the means? But neither Gilles nor Juliana was capable of evaluating the situation with such precision. Even though Gilles's mind was as clear as crystal and as sharp as a diamond, he was, above all, in the position of father and husband. As such he was like an eel on a toasting fork, his anguish too great to allow him the use of his normal powers of persuasion or his ordinarily impressive habit of detachment and objectivity. Juliana, meanwhile, had become a cluster, a mass of brooding apprehension, her understanding shrunk to a mere groan.

As time went on, Aurore's determination to have her own way became clearer and clearer. Had it not become simply a battle of wills between her and her parents and the actual reason for the argument forgotten in the desire for independence, obscured by fatigue and desperation? Aurore, in the first flush of youth and vitality, talked of the operation as though it were nothing – a mere detail to be forgotten in the light of a successful acting career. It would amount to no more than an hour of unconsciousness and a few days of discomfort in an irreproachable hospital or clinic. Afterwards the bliss of being different, of beginning a new existence unencumbered by an excrescence that she had, she said, never recognised as a part of herself, and had almost thought of as belonging to another – perhaps some ancestor who had, like the Bad

178

Fairy, bequeathed her a birthright she would have been happier without.

What some of their friends saw as strange was that, generally speaking, in all animals, including birds and even reptiles, the nose is the most sensitive and tender part of the anatomy, the most informative, the most crucially important for survival. Even if, in the course of several million years, its functions for human beings have diminished in usefulness, it still remains symbolically significant. If Aurore was ready to spite her face it was not that she was throwing out of the window something that was necessary to the human condition but instead it was her father's nose and symbolised her race and ancestry. This was of course the outsider's point of view and, for people such as Vivienne and her parents, she was rejecting what she had no right to reject. Aurore however saw her nose as alien and unwanted. Like the ugly duckling she longed for transformation and did not see why, in the context of the modern world with the acquired skills of modern science, she should be deprived of the opportunity for metamorphosis.

It was this that finally undermined Juliana's arguments and emotional pleas. Confronted by Aurore's claim for the recognition of her own destiny, the incontrovertible fact that her nose was her own and that she had every right to do what she liked with it, Juliana's objections fell to the ground. In conformity with the ideas of Monsieur and Madame Eckhardt and the intellectual circles she belonged to, Juliana could not, in the last resort, forbid an act so serious that was not her responsibility. Although she continued to feel that Aurore was about to deny, even desecrate an intimate link between them – since, as Aurore's mother, she must have had a part in the creation of that particular nose – she was at the same time the first to recognise Aurore's right to exercise free will as a guarantee of her individuality, a concept essential for becoming the successful actress that Aurore longed to be.

For Juliana the agony was extreme. She was full of premonition. The operation – in her eyes so unnatural – was bound to end badly. Why, she could not say, but the feeling was there, as strong as it was incommunicable. Gilles said what he was expected to say, that such a view was a piece of unnecessary foolishness, that she must not allow herself to be so pessimistic. Although unwilling to admit it, he too was uneasy and he resumed his role as chief supporter and comforter of his wife. Together heroically sticking to their conviction that everyone has a right to lead their lives as they wish, they coalesced into a single entity, a silent living protest, consenting against their will to an operation they considered, at its best, barbarous.

Chapter Eleven

Nina was growing up and, although in some ways I had less to do, I was more fully occupied at home than ever before. For some months I saw and heard little of the Deloiseaus. Juliana may have written, but her letters, although affectionate, were always phlegmatic, summary. She seldom let herself go in descriptions or flights of fancy, conveying only the bare bones of family events or developments. Ordinarily, this sufficed, since her very refusal to allow her imagination to run away with her – a habit that, in my family, was a normal indulgence – actually suggested a greater intimacy. From my knowledge of the background I could easily fill in all the details she left out.

At this time, however, perhaps she left out more than usual, more anyhow than I could possibly guess or imagine. The situation with regard to Aurore's nose had reached its climax. Aurore had won the day and an operation had been arranged in a very carefully chosen and distinguished clinic. But I only heard this from our elderly mutual friends Dorothy and Simon, Vivienne's parents, who were a part of all our lives. They telephoned to tell me there was a crisis. Aurore's heart had ceased to beat during the operation, and although, under the emergency treatment given by the surgeon, it had revived, Aurore remained in a coma. Juliana was in an indescribable state of mind and spent all her time at the clinic with Gilles, hoping for a change in Aurore's condition.

When I telephoned, she was amazingly calm, self-controlled and apparently dispassionate. She was able to tell me that she had always known something dreadful would happen – and in fact felt much as I did when my brother was killed. It was a state of mind common to everybody in such situations. She had sat in the waiting room for hours – far too long – before anyone came to tell her what had occurred. To her it seemed as though the anaesthetist had been at fault. The brain, too long starved of oxygen, was not yet functioning normally, but there was room for hope. Cases had been known where, after months of coma, people had recovered. Juliana and, as far as possible, Gilles, who was still working, spent all their time at Aurore's bedside. Tubes penetrated and extruded from her young body which lay inert, except for the fact, which now seemed miraculous, that you could see her breathing. Her heart continued to beat and so she was, to all intents and purposes, still alive – but that was all that could be said. Hope, if there at all, had faded to something artificial, kept alive only by Juliana's willpower.

This state of things continued for a long time – perhaps

a month or six weeks – when Juliana, seeing there was no improvement, insisted on removing Aurore from the clinic and taking her back to their apartment. She lay there in the care of a day nurse and a night nurse. Gilles and Juliana had become desperate. Unable to sit and do nothing, incredulous of the prognosis and advice of the medical doctors, they found a Japanese specialist, who prescribed an unusual diet – he advised that they pump rice into her youthful but emaciated body; she was growing thinner and thinner and less substantial, day by day.

I went to Paris with the sole intention of seeing Juliana, Gilles and, of course, Aurore. Now, as I rose in the old lift and rang the bell, waiting on that familiar staircase for Juliana to open the door, I could not help remembering the first time I had been there; recognising in the sound of Juliana's footsteps the same sound I had heard twenty years before. Nothing, it seemed, had changed – but the door opened, and there was my beloved Juliana, older, thinner, whiter although, barring a few grey hairs, not white-headed.

She took me into the other half of the salon. This was where she now lived, where she and Gilles ate and received their numerous visitors, from old friends to the newest quack doctor. Gilles was at work and we were alone. No noise came from the adjoining part of the room which was entirely devoted to Aurore. Juliana no doubt described the status quo and told me of the latest developments, such as they were – but I don't remember what they were. I only know she was, if in a state of inner anguish, outwardly calm and self-possessed. It was about three months after the operation, and still there was no real change in Aurore's condition. And it was only because they could see her heart beating they knew she was alive, and because, when Gilles spoke to her, tears poured down her cheeks.

Eventually Juliana took me in to see her. The room was in almost complete darkness. If the nurse was there, as she must have been, I was unaware of her presence. The bed had been placed in the middle of the available space, almost exactly where the dining-room table had once been. At its head were tall stands carrying tubes and other paraphernalia for maintaining the life that still inhabited the frail body that lay on the bed. I knew of course that it was Aurore. But she was unrecognisable. She was a tiny waxen image resembling nothing. Her nose, it is true, was prominent – but I could not tell whether or not it had been altered. And at that moment it did not even occur to me to ask. There was little or nothing I could say. The fact that though she was not dead she was still not alive overshadowed all other questions. And so I left Juliana to her misery, knowing that there was nothing I could do to alleviate it. It was too intimate, too personal and too desperate – a situation in which I, for the moment, had no role to play.

In trying to tell Vivienne's aunts back in England what I had seen, I found myself describing Aurore's body in such a way that shocked them as being over-emotional, and as I felt their disapproval, I agreed – but was unable to stop myself. Incapable of expressing my true feelings – for what were they alongside the appalling truth – I imitated my husband Edward, whose sympathy and warmth, although often exaggerated and sometimes embarrassing, were nearly always heartfelt. But I was now alone, and felt immediately that, in telling them that Aurore had lain there like a white ghost, I had made a faux pas. And so I had, since where, in such a sentence, was any true feeling for the actual and inescapable fact that Aurore was still alive, still there to give her parents a glimmer of hope even though she lacked all capacity to move or to speak?

But it was with regard to Nina that I mismanaged things. Feeling that she would be deeply upset if I broke the truth to her all at once, I told her merely that Aurore had had a very bad time of it in the clinic and that she was now extremely ill. Nina said little, but saw that there was more to it than that. I had succeeded only in making her anxious, and when later I told her of Aurore's death, she was hardly surprised. If she suffered, she kept her feelings to herself, unwilling to expose herself on the one hand to Edward's excesses or on the other to my mute sympathy, egocentric and unconvincing.

The operation had taken place in January. It was not until September that Aurore died. Tenderly cared for until the last breath, she was buried in the dreary little village cemetery in the country. I never saw her grave. I only knew that, after the sale of the house, Juliana continued to go there every so often to put flowers on it, believing as she did that Aurore, translated into another substance or medium, was still somehow there, able to play her part in the life she had abandoned.

Gilles and Juliana shrank. From being the warm and vital couple who welcomed their friends and the friends of those friends to share anything they had to offer, they became fragile, clinging to each other like two dark birds of the night, pursuing secret paths through the chaotic streets of Paris to find priests or anyone who could help them. Their health had suffered, and they too now needed the skills and support of doctors. Juliana, compelled by a deep need of life, became a little kinder to Gilles, while he did his best to satisfy her unspoken demands.

*   *   *

Juliana spent the next six years moving uneasily between her life with Gilles and her parents. She no longer painted, and no longer wrote – she had written a little book of *mémoires* destined for Aurore. A dark, solitary if benevolent figure, she travelled on the train which, in those days, took seven hours to reach its destination in the south, where she found herself back in the world of her childhood. Here the sun purged her of self-pity, reducing her to one among so many women who had lost all that was dearest to them. She learned to pray, to accept, and gradually to come to terms with her fate.

She had so wished to hand on to Aurore the taste, the atmosphere, the emotions of her past, and so had written her account without any idea of publication or renown. But, as a woman brought up with books, with a sense of the value of words and all they can express, she wrote a passable prose which, while not being of the first order, still conveyed a vivid feeling of her own childhood. Now, in the absence of any such stimulant, she couldn't help thinking of those early times and their blissful sense of innocence and joy.

It was Juliana's mouth that seemed to express all her passions and pleasures, either laughing with amusement or drooping with childish disgust. She had suffered from some allergy or weakness – I could not remember exactly what – the only remedy for which was to deny her any form of sweet or patisserie. She was brought up on a strict diet, and trailed past shop windows with her tongue hanging out and her eyes glued to the cakes shining with brilliant red cherries or puffing out glorious clouds of whipped cream. Neither was she allowed to accept presents from well-meaning friends. As such gifts were often made on the spur of the moment, she could remember when she was obliged to sit and watch others enjoying delicacies intended for her. When very young she grew painfully to understand that wanting, however badly, does not necessarily mean you can have – and perhaps this was salutary. At any rate her love for her parents never wavered, and grew into a caring, protective love without a shadow of resentment, for she knew they had always done their best for her.

All this and much more went through Juliana's mind in those years when her heart seemed frozen, unable to feel, just as her mind was unable to think. From time to time she abandoned Gilles, leaving him to look after himself in that Paris they both now found unsympathetic. But they decided on one thing together, and that was to move from Auteuil to St-Germain, where I had always hoped they would one day live. They left behind them the memory of that small white body fighting a losing battle for life, which faded into something manageable, something that only claimed attention in the dark hours, or when you were told of other cases of the same kind. Juliana, while not forgetting, contained the memory, incomprehensible though it was, and the strength of her own past vitality reasserted itself.

It was now that she conceived the idea of adopting a little boy. A little girl would have been a temptation for the devil – but a little boy meant something new and deeply refreshing. Juliana and Gilles made enquiries, and finally found a little boy of about two years old whose parents had deserted him. He was called Michel, and proved himself to be intelligent and affectionate. In adopting him Juliana felt she had done something painful but essential. She had deflected her own mind from thinking eternally about what might have been, about a daughter she had adored, a life she had once had, which would never return. She devoted herself to Michel – and Michel rewarded her with his innocence, his desire to live his life. Having never known Aurore, he was untainted, unmarked and blissfully egotistical.

One could have said, at moments, that Gilles suffered more than Juliana did. But he immersed himself in work, investing himself over and beyond his work as a civil servant, organising meetings, corresponding with people of all sorts and nationalities, inviting them for interviews in his study to discuss his plans for reforming education. It was this huge subject that had suddenly absorbed him, helping him to forget his daughter and to plunge himself into an impersonal project. Or, putting on his overcoat and taking with him his shabby briefcase, he would say: '*Au revoir, chérie,*' or '*A toute à l'heure,*' and disappear, having shut the heavy door behind him and, in too much of a rush to wait for the lift, would hurry down the red-carpeted stairs. He needed Juliana's support. For her he had no secrets and, when he returned, the discussions between them would last for hours. He would recount to her in detail his propositions, ideas and ideals, just as he always had. For men like Gilles were becoming rare. His integrity, his sense of justice or truth were bound to provoke, to perturb – and so he was also bound to struggle and fight for everything he believed in. He became greyer, thinner, less and less connected with everyday life. Always gentle, benevolent in his own way, and full of good intentions, he left behind him a trace of asperity, of rigour, his reactions always intense and exalted and, for me, often lacking that essential sympathy I so craved.

This I found with Juliana and, to my subsequent shame, we often talked lightly of Gilles, in patronising terms, as though able to see him from the outside only, blind to what he might be feeling. Even Juliana was not entirely guiltless in this respect, implying a distance between Gilles and herself which, in spite of loyalty and devotion, had grown larger with time.

Warm, generous and motherly, Juliana dominated her small society. The apartment filled like a bucket with friends and dependants – both the young who had nowhere to stay and perhaps too little to eat, or the elderly who, having always known her, came back again and again. The apartment was superb and had a view from above on to the flying buttresses of St-Germain-des-Prés. A passage wound round to the back where a miserable dark space did duty for a kitchen, a section of which had been cut off to make room for a maid's bedroom. There were also two attractive rooms up a flight of steps above Gilles's bedroom, which were hardly used, in spite of the fact they would have made an ideal studio for Juliana, where she could have worked uninterrupted by the comings and goings that took place below. She had no very convincing answer to my question as to why she did not do this. No doubt, if there was one, it lay in her own personality, and it was true that I could not imagine her retreating to such a private place, out of bounds to all save the most intimate friends. She would not then have been able to dominate everything that happened in the apartment, constantly exercising her judgement and common sense on all the incidents that arose in daily life either between her and Gilles, or with a *bonne à tout faire* who came two or three times a week, and was known as le Dragon, or with the electrician, the carpenter, or

Gilles's distinguished friends. All this, it is true, she would have greatly missed, and would certainly have thought everything less well managed had she not been there to do it herself.

It was strange how the apartment took on almost immediately the same atmosphere as their previous one. The divided sitting room, with its white silk curtains heavily hanging in the winter or, in the summer when the windows were open, fluttering lightly inwards, and the accordion-pleated screen, which could be used to divide the room in two, the grand piano, behind which so many canvases were stacked as though to await the day of judgement – all was so much the same, so familiar, that each time I came to stay I returned to a relationship that had not really changed, where I was again only sixteen and Juliana half friend, half mother.

A full-length picture of Aurore, dressed for going out, hung in a corner. Every time I went along the corridor, I came face to face with it. And every time I remembered that what I saw as my 'treachery' still lay, an unsolved puzzle, at the bottom of my heart. Why had I tried to stop Aurore from becoming what she most wanted to be – an actress? For some reason, I did not think of confessing to Juliana. But as long as I persisted in my silence I would continue to feel guilty. Although the picture recalled Aurore and was, in a way, very like her, I privately thought it was a bad picture. It was scrubby and unconvincing – a dream picture, satisfying perhaps for Juliana and Gilles, but without true sensuality or visual existence. It was a travesty of Aurore, her vitality, radiance and charm – in itself it was nothing. And slowly it took its place as part of the decor, a reminder only of what had once been.

It was the serried ranks of books on the shelves that gave distinction to the rooms. There were books everywhere, and most of the great works of literature, both French and English, could be found among them. In the midst of this order and muddle and after six years' paralysis, Juliana started to paint again. Her work had changed from the old days, becoming more abstract. On a small scale, and in pastel, these pictures reflected her pain and anguish in long, narrow shapes like skyscrapers or the tails of comets. They were obsessive, even unpleasant, with one intention only – but here I paused, unable to say what that was. But yes, I knew that Juliana felt as though she were in the dark, and these pictures might help to change the decor.

There was of course much that I didn't know – much that I only heard about, like the new house somewhere in the west, in the flat lands cut through by canals, reflecting, in Juliana's pictures, orange trees and small, mother-of-pearl clouds. I never went there and only briefly met the cousin who made this venture possible. It was evident that Juliana needed to get away from Paris, with its noise, bad air and struggle for existence, but also from Gilles, who again lived a life of great intensity, concentrated on a vision that, although interesting, was both idealistic and depressive. I remembered how, on my first encounter with him, he had reminded me of an eastern prince. Time had worn away the glamour to reveal a man honed to a state of admirable integrity. In his work, often itself invented and self-imposed, he constantly rubbed up against the worldly and ambitious – even more disconcertingly against those with ulterior motives who could not, in the long run, be trusted. They came up against his steely inflexibility which, in growing stronger with age, had no need of any but the approval and support of Juliana. She was perhaps warmer, more sympathetic, more imaginative, but Gilles, in a few words, invariably put everything in its place. Truth, often unpalatable, became incontrovertible. And those who sought it showed their true mettle either by acceptance or, occasionally, rejection.

Juliana progressed even now like a ship in full sail but, as my own life came apart, I saw less of her. Still, she exercised an influence. When I talked of my indecision in leaving Edward because I had no other lover within sight, Juliana pointed out that surely every woman had as much right to a life of her own as any man. She could be, like a plant, a single species, growing alone until, one day, she found somebody. I hardly knew what I was doing or what I wanted, but had cut loose, and now felt a longing to be alone. I had to think things out – and went to stay in an old house in the Dordogne. There I began to take stock of my situation, of how I had spent the best years of my life staying at home, looking after my children – eventually to feel dissatisfied with myself. Now, what else was there? I could not answer the question, but came back feeling calmer.

I came through Paris to find Juliana more like she used to be, living the same sort of life she had always lived. Aurore was not often mentioned by either of her parents. When this happened, however, it was with the greatest naturalness, without self-consciousness or self-pity. Neither Gilles nor Juliana were sentimental snivellers; they bore their misfortune with dignity – and that was all there was to be said. New life, new needs and new youth took Aurore's place. Grateful for Juliana's hospitality, girls came to stay and to help, and were welcomed like lost children. They rewarded Juliana with affection and gratitude unless, as happened in one or two cases, they resented her maternal grasp, her amazing certainty about what they ought to do. In those cases they eluded her dominance but often, being for some reason or other dependent, they remained impressed, even friendly. No one could say that Juliana was possessive, and aware of their resistance she would not resent the girls' independence and would continue to be as helpful as she had always been. If she suffered from a sense of failure she did not show it, and remained strong enough to tolerate such differences.

One of the people they occasionally saw was Bruno. He had married, and now had six children. Of these, there was one who I made friends with – a girl, dark and elegant. Bruno too had fined down, perhaps as a consequence of having married a gifted and intelligent woman, who taught the piano and became very friendly with Juliana. As for Bruno, he continued to do the same sort of work as before and lived in Nimes, where, very occasionally, I went to see them.

I had a major operation and took quite a long time to recover. I did not see Juliana nearly so often, but she wrote and, as I now see on re-reading them, her letters began to betray a certain weakness and fatigue. She wanted me to find her books by young English writers, saying that she was sick of French writing – it had become mediocre. I was badly informed but sent a few suggestions. Juliana read and criticised them, and was attracted by one – a young man who, later, did not develop as she had hoped. And we thought up an idea of spending a short holiday together in the Lake District with our paintboxes. Meanwhile Juliana had a large retrospective exhibition in Belgium. She said the gallery was beautiful, but she was feeling too exhausted to go – it was Gilles who did all the necessary work. Juliana retired to bed, defeated by an immense fatigue which she could trace to nothing in particular. And a later letter – probably the last she ever wrote to me – described her condition as bedridden and exhausted. In these circumstances she could not contemplate a holiday in England.

I did not at first understand. I may even have protested and said that a holiday would do her good. That, of course, was foolish of me. But I did not know then what it meant to be old – to be in a condition when death could not be far off, and where her fatigue seemed to express, independently of her will, her true condition. Whereas, in the past, she had been someone who breathed life into everything around her through the richness of her mind and the warmth of her manner, now this richness and warmth had faded. There were signs of some old weakness to be found near her heart, as in a fruit that has waited too long in the studio for the painter to finish the picture. Still relatively young and having just recovered from a life-threatening illness, I felt inclined to resent her

197

seeming negativity – I suppose I felt it was spoiling my fun. Moreover I could not face a life without Juliana. She was still a bulwark, a gift, a kind of insurance against the mediocrity of the world, something that I could not conceive of being without. She represented the old world, the ancient civilisation, the once rich enjoyment.

Eventually, hearing that Juliana was in hospital, I went to Paris. The memory of that visit is too poignant to be entirely forgotten. Juliana in her hospital bed could have been straight out of a picture by Degas. Her hair, still only streaked with grey, hung on her neck. Her night-dress and the sheets were of that extraordinary white that comes of using pastel, and the little table by the bed was laden with bottles and an uneaten bowl of soup – a still life. Juliana complained that Gilles, anxious to do his best, brought her too much to eat. She had no appetite and knew that for him it was a waste of time – he could not boil an egg – how silly! It weighed on her. She described her illness. She knew roughly what was wrong. Perhaps she guessed more but did not want to upset me. Or perhaps also she did not very much care. After an hour I left her lying back on her pillows, calm but exhausted. 'Oh! *Ma petite Agnès, que je suis fatiguée.*' On her lips this meant not only her present condition, but her whole life. I never saw her again.

Aurore

When the telephone rang in London, where I was then living, I was hardly surprised to hear Gilles's voice telling me that Juliana had died the night before. I wrote to say that, if he wanted me to, I would go and help him – and oddly enough I seem to have been the only person to have made such an offer. Gilles was touched and never forgot it. On my side I was less devastated than I expected to be. Having absorbed the news, I did not react to it. I was conscious only of an indescribable blank, as when you have lost something important but can't quite remember what it was.

Chapter Twelve

Though Juliana had disappeared, Gilles was still very much there. And Juliana's absence made Gilles's presence stand out like a solitary beacon. He never failed me. He sincerely thought of me as someone worthwhile, which gave a boost to my self-confidence. When I now went to Paris, I stayed in the apartment where, for a time, he continued to live. The sense of muddle and confusion persisted. Inevitably it had become more his scene than hers. It was he who now occupied the main salon, and whose numerous and unclassifiable papers flowed over the huge table, burying themselves unaccountably beneath each other, lost, then re-discovered and lost again. Their nature varied from purely humdrum bills and accounts to philosophical essays to be read aloud in the summer, at intellectual reunions in the country, or the very individual, concise and personal poetry that issued at moments from Gilles like the song of the nightingale.

Occasionally he read these aloud to me. He read well, in the style of the Comédie Française. I couldn't of course emulate him, though once, I remembered, he came in to find me in the act of reading aloud one of his poems in my weak voice and uncertain accent and, striding towards me with unconscious masculine superiority –

which made him for the moment immensely attractive
– he seized the book from me and read aloud himself,
dominating me, authoritative and convincing. I didn't
understand a word, and only remembered that I must
trump up some sort of reaction – difficult, since I hadn't
been moved, as I ought to have been, by that noble, and
least definable of all the arts, poetry.

When I stayed with him, I often did the shopping.
Gilles would give me the money out of the drawer where
Juliana had always kept it – a source that never seemed
to dry up, and I supposed that, on receiving his monthly
salary, Gilles renewed the supply as he always had, for
them both to draw on in case of need. It had been like
that in the past, and had always impressed me by its
simplicity and lack of nonsense, its sense of trust and
fundamental dignity. It reminded me too of the same
innocent, albeit less transparent spirit that animated my
parents in their weekly struggle with the financial aspects
of life – ludicrous perhaps but necessary and inescapable.
Pennies, farthings and halfpennies had then to be
accounted for – and, because they hadn't the clarity of
mind to put a supply of cash in a drawer, they did their
accounts. Painstakingly and not without a kind of enjoyment, they accounted for packets of cigarettes, or shared
the expenses of going to the cinema. So was their relationship confirmed.

Gilles, having decided on his new habits, his new diet – different from that when Juliana was alive – had also decided on the shops he had confidence in. Meat and fish were to be bought, but only at a certain butcher or fishmonger, just as yogurt and potatoes were to be had at a health food shop further up the street, and bread, of extreme importance, at a particular new bakery situated near the boulevard where, because of the immense variety in shape and size, and the delicious smell that emanated from the doorway, there was always a queue.

I enjoyed my shopping and the subsequent cooking, although Gilles had become intractable in the restrictions he insisted on. He had always eaten the food provided by Juliana and, because he admired everything she did, had assumed her cooking to be excellent. But he thought of food simply as a means of re-fuelling, not for enjoyment. He knew he needed to eat, but had Juliana offered him pills, he would have been perfectly content. He was always in a feverish state to get on with his work and, while munching on some delicious morsel cooked by her, would analyse and hypothesise about the next item on his list. He would look at his watch three or four times during a meal, wipe his lips immediately on finishing his plateful and, rising at once, would leave the table to return to his study. In the end, Juliana would be glad to see him go. Although he was a good conversationalist and had his own brand of humour, a marvellous memory and always knew what was going on and, when they had a sympathetic guest, could exert all his charm, he was a drag.

For me, who came to France to enjoy its cooking and the extraordinary *sérieux* with which the French regarded their food, Gilles's indifference was hard to take. Now that he was alone, however, and had to do everything for himself, I could only admire the energy with which he confronted problems that were new to him, and the thoroughness and method with which he dealt with them. Juliana had died of cancer of the liver due, as he thought, to her style of cooking – succulent legs of lamb, served with delicious sauté potatoes, for instance. Having watched her die in her narrow hospital bed, he was determined not to finish his life in the same way, and had therefore adopted a Spartan dietary regime that abhorred all fat. He even put saccharine pills into his coffee and so, of course, grew thinner and thinner. This suited him however. He became greyer and a little shabbier, but, partly because his clothes had been of excellent quality in the first place, remained elegant. His silhouette was that of a man about town, elderly, old-fashioned and distinguished. A dreamer, a cogitator – in short, an intellectual – he walked through the crowded streets thinking his own particular thoughts, as though he were in his study. But although his mind was evidently on other things, his contact with people on buses or in shops remained excellent. His manners were impeccable. He created a very favourable impression when he lifted his homburg to a lady, and when he insisted, at the butcher's, on a particularly lean cut of meat, his requests were always honoured as far as possible. When I did the shopping I had only to say the name, Monsieur Deloiseau, to be given exactly what I had asked for, even when it had to be fetched from cold storage.

The first time I went to Paris after Juliana's death, I wondered what I would find – not only how Juliana's death would have affected Gilles personally (this, I was sure, would be devastatingly apparent), but how he was filling his time since he was now retired from the Cour des comptes. Filled with certain assumptions of my youth, I could imagine nothing better than Gilles becoming a full-time poet! Little did I know of the claims of the poetic muse.

I was, I remember, shocked by Gilles's decision (one that, it became immediately evident, there was no hope of changing) to devote himself entirely to rehabilitating – or, rather, establishing as though from scratch – his wife's artistic reputation. I had set my heart on his fulfilling his own destiny now there was nothing standing in his way. But I was distorting a situation I had no real means of understanding. I was thinking, as my own family had always thought, in terms of the ego. I seemed to have forgotten that Gilles was bound to Juliana by love, yet I had assumed that he would now want to satisfy his own desires. I did not realise that his had long ago been purified, and become incandescent, like a blue flame whose purpose was, in the end, to evaporate.

Gilles proved himself to be an astute and efficient organiser. He created a Society of Friends of Juliana (in France a normal procedure, a kind of recognised protest against the all too powerful establishment), which eventually became financially solvent and was therefore able to bargain with various public museums and galleries. He organised shows of Juliana's outside Paris, one of which I attended. It was in Toulouse. After a journey across the centre of France of about seven hours, I finally arrived in a state of fatigue so great I could hardly walk from the hotel to the restaurant where we were all to have dinner. Nevertheless, feeling better after I had washed and brushed my hair, I found Gilles, Michel and several other friends sitting round a table, where I was able to disappear and forget myself. Michel talked about Juliana and the paintings, which we were to see the following day, and a German art dealer, a woman, seemed tempted to buy several. On seeing the show, I was impressed by the cool dignity of Juliana's work so that, after a time, it was not only loved by a small band of enthusiasts among whom were those who had actually known her and who claimed a certain recognition for their old and esteemed friend, but it was also recognised independently for its own merits.

Since Juliana had belonged to that generation that rather dreaded any sort of public recognition, Gilles had uphill work. Painting itself was changing so fast that Juliana's pictures seemed, from a superficial perspective, to be unrelated to modernity. And yet it was of course for this very reason that they were so refreshing and that people, once they had really looked at them, tended to greet them as they might an old friend, that particular quality which, for those who knew her, spelled her most characteristic, intimate self.

On my periodic visits to Paris, I found Gilles up to his neck in one thing or another – either an exhibition in a town like Toulouse or in the *Catalogue Raisonné* of Juliana's work that he had begun to compile. Only once or twice did he give me a brief recital of his own poetry. He told me that it came to him automatically, that he never 'tried' to write poetry but that it appeared, ready-made, in his mind. I thought of him rather like an old tree shooting forth at intervals tender twigs and branchlets. I hoped that one day his tree might be recognised for its own sake. But his modesty was too great. It created a kind of barrier beyond which few people ventured. Within it however Gilles remained himself, his integrity undiminished, his purpose a secret one. He published a couple of small volumes, one of which had seen the light during Juliana's lifetime. And I remembered that Juliana had, very unexpectedly, asked me to illustrate one of them. I had done my best and was not very proud of it. It was of children playing in the Jardins du Luxembourg, a little reminiscent of Boutet de Monvel. Finally, however, they were rejected by Juliana – she thought she would like to try her hand. I said nothing, but was a little annoyed by the peremptory gesture. Did Juliana think I didn't count – or were the drawings good enough to produce in her a certain jealousy, a feeling that, as Gilles's wife, she should be the one to illustrate his work? I never asked, since too many answers, none of them true, would have been forthcoming. And now that Juliana was dead, it was far more difficult to ask Gilles whether I could try again.

Occasionally during a meal in the kitchen, or when I returned from some cultural expedition, Gilles would suddenly spout a poem in its entirety without hesitation or making a mistake, as though reading from an invisible book. I rarely understood the words I heard. They were too dense, too philosophical. Nonetheless I felt they were poetry. I responded to the spirit rather than the actual text, and wasn't too shy to ask for an explanation, which Gilles would give readily enough. For him each word had its own, dense meaning, each phrase followed the other logically, and the whole represented something that was, for him, a greater reality than anything that I was capable of experiencing then. The magic of his inspiration was for me immensely impressive, even daunting, given I struggled all the time, and doubted myself to a degree that was shameful. I realised that, for Gilles, it was not – or was not any longer – a question of ambition. This had been dissolved years ago.

By now I had my own life. Separated from Edward, I frequently used Gilles's apartment when I was in Paris. There was always a bed for me there, and I was free to organise my time as I wanted, repaying Gilles by doing the shopping. I immensely enjoyed his concentration on his work – with him always the first consideration – and his readiness to enjoy simple pleasures, such as going to the cinema. I was amazed when I found that he loved Sean Connery, for example, and realised that I had, without knowing it, restricted Gilles's interests more than he deserved. For him these films were exercises of ingenuity, a sort of game in which it was very amusing to see not who, since this was always the 'goodies', but how they won. To my own romantic mind this added a new dimension. I learned how to be amused for the sake of being amused, and enormously enjoyed our evenings out.

I often wished I lived nearer to him, close enough to drop in and sit at the kitchen table, enjoy a coffee and the trenchant, even brilliant conversation he provided. He was concerned, for the most part, with ideas or whether one believed in a sense of values or happiness as, according to Gilles, Juliana had, but about which he himself was very sceptical. I was wrong, however, in thinking our choice of subjects was always abstract and theoretical; our conversations were often full of common sense and useful information, especially instructive about historical details, such as the habits of Proust, or those of Gilles's own grandfather. Laughter was there too, even if rarefied and unsensual, the fruit of knowledge and wit rather than that of cakes and ale. But how I loved sitting there, forced to defend my own rather flimsy ideas from Gilles's hummingbird interjections, often voiced before I had finished my sentence. It was sometimes hard to believe he really listened to what I said. But months later he would occasionally repeat a conversation or recall an idea of mine, even complimenting me on my intentions, thus showing he both heard and remembered, adding a mite to my hard-won store of self-confidence.

One day, coming in on a summer evening from some such outing, Gilles turned and seized me round the waist.

I should perhaps have expected such a thing, since Gilles constantly complimented me on my appearance. But I had not. It was one of my greatest failings that I did not even try to be sexy – at least not with Gilles – and was therefore little in the habit of producing or receiving sexual advances. And Gilles stank of tobacco, which made him unattractive. He tried hard to kiss me – but found me unprepared and unwilling. Flashing back, I saw myself at the age of seventeen in the other apartment. Coming down from my *chambre de bonne* one day, I had just entered the back door and was passing the lavatory, when the door opened and Gilles emerged, still buttoning his flies. He looked at me and apologised, turning away to finish what he was doing. I was embarrassed, and fled to the salon, swallowing my emotions which, of course, never came to anything – hiding the thought that here was, after all, an attractive man. Had Gilles been unprincipled – this was unthinkable – or less in love with Juliana, he could have made short work of me during the six months I spent living under the same roof. My family may have feared for my virtue, but in fact ignorance and inexperience were my greatest protection. Added to my timidity they were a more effective barrier to sexual licence than any amount of knowledge or awareness.

And now – well, although I felt love and affection for Gilles, time had intervened. I managed to stall Gilles's advances with kindness and some show of reason, while he said he needed a woman and that he was sexually frustrated – also that the last year or so with Juliana had been extraordinary. They had, it seemed, re-experienced all the ardour of their youth. And now he could not bear the gap that yawned. He said also that he thought of himself as '*un homme tragique*' – a man of tragedy! I was deeply shocked. 'Everyone,' I said, 'has tragedy in their lives – everyone. You are no different, no more special than those others, many of whom suffer every day from a situation prolonged apparently beyond endurance. Your tragedy is now a thing of the past. What you should do now is to live – but not, however, with me.' Gilles was impressed, and capitulated with all his native grace. I was saddened, but knew it was better so. Gilles was too intellectual, I too intuitive.

So Gilles concentrated on Juliana's art, putting every ounce of energy into the catalogue. By and by he no longer felt the need for a woman in his life, and it was evident to me that it was just as well I had not said yes to his demands. His admiration for Juliana blossomed anew and was translated into a book illustrated by her paintings. In it were all the early, religious paintings that were the first I remembered – the ones that hung on the walls of the apartment in Auteuil, and which I had always looked at with, as it were, half an eye averted. There were also the thick, heavy paintings of the south, in which there were no figures, and, later, there were smaller paintings of the skies of the north. Juliana's personality disengaged itself and was presented through Gilles's exertions as something remarkable. I wondered what it was I had so loved; that is to say, how could I put it into words? What was it these black lines expressed, and these curiously clumsy trees and thick-walled houses? And yet, though they were in a way not beautiful at all, I found them deeply moving.

Gilles was self-sufficient. He worked as hard as ever, and that gave him confidence. He relinquished his claims on me while at the same time needing me. His distinction meant nothing to me. I had suffered all my life from the renown and unworldliness of my elders and betters, and if, as I still hoped, I was now to have a life of my own, I must shun, escape or ruthlessly forget them. Yet Gilles and I continued as it were on parallel lines and, when we met at breakfast or dinner, signalled to each other as though in Morse, to compare notes about our day's experiences.

Eventually Gilles moved to yet another apartment, in another district. This time, it was his own choice. Again, romantic as ever, I had hoped he would choose, for example, the rue Mouffetard, or the Quai Montebello –

but he was determined not to be romantic, and in any case the rents were too high. He found an apartment near the avenue de Suffren, an apartment on the third floor with no view to speak of. But it was protected, quiet, clean and small. The money that came from selling the other one he gave to Michel, who had become a photographer. There were only two rooms besides the kitchen – and when I stayed, as I did once or twice, I slept in the living room.

It was here that he reproved me for cooking roast potatoes in butter and showed me how much better it was to do them without fat, so that they became brown and rather hard. Quite often he would take me out to a restaurant round the corner, where I always had sole meunière, and he a lamb chop. He had grown thinner and greyer, but we remained affectionate and intimate, all the time conscious of a past that had somehow shaped and tuned us, like old instruments found in a corner, and for a moment brought back to life. He was never boring, and I lapped up his wisdom, and even his misunderstanding which had in the past, I remembered, irritated me.

We talked of books, of films, of my new house in the south – of everything except politics. And one day I invited him to stay. But instead of staying in my house he stayed in the local hotel on the corner, from where he walked slowly up the hill to arrive on my doorstep for lunch. Once here he relaxed, spent the afternoon in the garden – which was looking very beautiful just then – and walked back again in time for bed.

In a quiet way he enjoyed himself and even talked of coming to live here. I was relieved when he finally went back to Paris and the care of Michel, in whose arms he did eventually die. This was my last contact with the old world, and left me feeling cold, as though owing a debt I could never repay. There was, of course, no happy end. Gilles always said that whereas Juliana believed in happiness, he had never been able to. And perhaps he was right. Like outdated music in a minor key, it is beautiful, but you can see, or rather hear, the skeletons rattling their bones in the distance.

Postscript

Jealousy, as was well known in medieval times, is one of the worst of sins. But it does not attack without first being encouraged, and the seedbed from which it arises is, above all, a lack of self-confidence. Had I been aware, or more aware, of what was going on in my *for intérieur*, I might have been able to vanquish this monster, that, like some wily serpent, insinuated itself between my dreams of affection and love, and wrought something so dark and poisonous as to be unmentionable. It was because it was never talked of, no doubt, that it had the power to hurt both the victim and the other person, that is to say me, and that finally the pain and a growing sense of responsibility helped me to see myself with some sort of reason and reasonableness, and shed this monster that was on the point of devouring me. But this process of understanding took a very long time, and the mists only cleared away long after Aurore had died.

I wrote the first version of this piece for the Memoir Club, started, it is said, by Molly McCarthy in the 1920s in the hope of persuading her husband Desmond to produce a novel or some other more ambitious piece of work. Naturally, it failed – but the club survived and I, though much the youngest member, was tolerated rather as a child born on the wrong side of the blanket is tolerated, simply because it cannot be helped. This, however, is the only paper I ever read. The only comment I remember was I think by Desmond McCarthy, who was surprised that I could recall so many details. But as a *mémoire* it did not fail. I am not sure what date this was, but I stopped before Aurore became grown up, and have therefore added a lot to it since. It has actually been almost entirely rewritten, but these facts account for its existence and it has taken me nearly twenty years to write, inhibited perhaps by the existence of Gilles, who didn't die until the late nineties.

I have been asked by a friend who knew them to restore their real names. But I refused, having already re-christened them, I think rather well, to suit their personalities, and also in an effort to put them in the distance, so that I should not find myself crushed by their presence, unable to think of them with a certain detachment.

Their real names were Sylvie, Zoum and François Walter, just as Madame Eckhardt's name was Jeanne Vanden Eckhoudt. If I put them at a distance it does not mean hiding them – but they are all four now under the earth and will not complain of such treatment. Indeed if I thought they were within hearing, I would long ago have knelt in front of Sylvie, and have asked her pardon – and, having done so, would probably not have written this memoir.

The Birthday Party

His hands, almost transparent, blue with the chill of extreme old age, lay on the coverlet, tips of fingers placed together, as in Buddhist prayer. They had lost their old capacity to dance a descriptive arabesque, cigarette held between index and middle fingers. Instead of gracefully describing, they acquiesced in passivity, like the hands on an alabaster tomb. In his face, the colour of mother-of-pearl, his nose still asserted its robust, eighteenth-century shape. On the top of his fine, silver-sprinkled hair was a woollen cap knitted in many colours, and his feet, protruding from under the blanket, were sheathed in striped woollen socks. On one of them perched a canary, which he was perhaps now looking at. His regard was oblique and one could not be sure.

Someone passed in the passage outside, looked in for an instant to see that all was well, and went downstairs to let in the sound of children's voices. 'Can I, oh can we – may we see him? Can we just say hello? After all, it's our house! We want to welcome him.' And another voice, steady, calming: 'You must wait a little. He's asleep now . . . later on, later.' And the tumult of voices, the rushing of small, energetic feet, so confident of goodwill, was all at once shut out by the banging of a door.

But the canary had been disturbed. It flew to the top of the rubber tree, the yellow of its wings reflected for a brief moment on the ceiling. The eyes of the old man did not follow it, but soon saw it again, perched on the other foot. He sighed, whether from contentment or otherwise, it was difficult to say.

There was a wheelchair in one corner of the room, a small table on which there was a block of watercolour paper and some brushes and tubes of paint; also a tumbler of water. A little canvas was propped up, showing a beginning: some red and blue splashes, some dribbles where the paint had run down. It was tentative, but one could see that it had a firm intention behind it. All round the walls there were pictures, and still more stacked in the corners. Plants and pictures – and books too in glass cases, well cared for, in good order.

The canary flew again, landing on one of the bookcases, dropping its liquid white excrement on to one of the tables below. Nothing else moved. There was no sound. It was as quiet as it is perhaps on the moon. But it was not cold; the room was full of warmth and affection. It was waiting simply – for what was not yet clear.

On the bed he hardly moved; sometimes sleeping, sometimes blinking his pale blue eyes that must at one time have been so large and so round. Now one could not be sure how much and how far they could see, and it was possible to imagine that, for him, the whole world was a conglomeration of blue, red and yellow dots, sometimes trickling or swimming together like marbled paper. Suddenly the eyes, a little glued up with the excretion of old age, opened wider: the canary had burst into song. It was twittering and chirruping and spilling out cascades of unpredictable notes in sudden ecstasy at something unknowable. It was evident that the old fellow on the bed enjoyed it; he brought the tips of his fingers together in a little peak, and turned his head an inch or two towards the sound. But the bird was out of sight, behind a leaf of the abutilon that grew in the bay window. Perhaps it was the sudden gleam of pale sunlight that had set it off.

The day was drawing in. There was the sound of deliberate footsteps, the clinking of cups and saucers, a reassuring hint of teatime. The door opened and in came Swallow, his friend, bearing a tray with a teapot on it and the cups. 'How are you feeling, Mischa? Want some tea?' and, putting the tray down on a chair, he took hold of the old man under his armpits, and sat him up against the pillows, as though he were Petrouchka.

But Petrouchka smiled: 'Whisky perhaps?' he said interrogatively.

Swallow laughed. 'Mischa, you old rogue,' he said, 'I'll put some in the tea. Then it will be Irish tea: you'll like that.'

221

Mischa laughed, very softly, wickedly, while Swallow poured in the whisky, and put the cup in Mischa's hand. But his fingers were not strong enough to hold it; tea and whisky spilled on to the sheet. 'Oh dear!' he lamented, without really meaning it. 'Never mind,' he said, without quite meaning that either.

Swallow wiped away the worst of it and held the cup to Mischa's lips. He blew on the tea, intending to suck it in, and laughed again at his failure. 'Mischa, suck,' said Swallow authoritatively.

So he sucked, learning the trick quite fast. The whisky went down, what was left of it, like a treat. He leaned back on his pillows and sighed again, quietly contented.

'And what will happen next?' he suddenly asked, as though out of the blue, just an idea that had occurred.

'Mischa, you know quite well: it's your birthday party this evening. People are coming. Nettie has made some wonderful food.'

'Oh! I had forgotten . . . so I shall have to get dressed, and make conversation?'

'Yes. But you have no need to worry. I shall dress you. And you know how to entertain people.'

Mischa lay back, evidently considering whether he could do this. For himself he was someone else: but he knew no one was likely to be able to understand such an idea. It was altogether too complicated.

222

The Birthday Party

Later on the children came in, squeezing shyly through the doorway, excited because they hadn't seen him before, this very old gentleman who had come to live in their house. What difference would he make to their lives? Mischa was interested. He distinguished a thin girl, her fair, greenish pigtails hanging inert down her back: as he expected, the race of little girls had not changed in eighty years. There were white socks on all those fidgeting feet; above them knobby knees, unconscious of their similarity to those of ponies, trembling in a field. Mischa held out his hand, as though to show by the gentleness of his gesture the full extent of his friendliness. It seemed to surprise, perhaps intimidate them, and their readiness to smother him in their desire to share their delight in life was momentarily paralysed. The girl touched his fingers with a formal politeness, and stood there, smiling a wan, embarrassed smile, while the two little boys stared, wondering and dumb. The canary, not to be left out, nearly had them laughing again by settling on the shoulder of one of them. But Swallow shooed them out, vaguely suggesting homework or bed, and they went, relieved. Mischa was rather disappointed: was he too old for such encounters?

But, he thought, I was once like them, though I was a lonely little boy with neither brother nor sister. Only I had my ayah, whom I loved, and needed no one else, really. She was so quiet, she had no self, only the desire to be everything to me; it would be nice if she were here now. When I was sent home at the age of seven, I wept – and so did she. I don't remember much but the whiteness of everything, especially the things she washed; and all the colours of the whites on the walls, and my mother's velvet dress, put on for parties. He seemed to float over those vast countries, India and Burma, bound in the far distance by the Himalayas, where there was a bear that had eaten his aunt. How his friends always laughed when he told that story, though there was nothing to it, nothing but this bizarre, surrealist fact, that she had been seized – and supposed eaten. Darkness descended. Someone came in to draw the blinds, and an unconscionable time passed – immeasurable, void. He was woken by Swallow, come to dress him for the party.

He sat in his wheelchair, his rainbow cap still on his head, a dark suit hiding his bones and a rug laid over his knees. His hands, now steadier, held a glass of whisky-on-the-rocks, and he was surrounded by a little group of people, talking more to each other than to him, joking and giggling. He regarded them with utter detachment, as though he were sitting at the summit of a mountain, and they were playing a game in the fields below. Sometimes he contributed a remark, eliciting much amusement, but, though pleased, the laughter seemed to him to have little connection with what he had said. His eyes gazed at the blurred world in the far corner of the room. 'Who is that over there?' he said, in wondering tones.

'Oh, that woman,' said a friend after turning briefly round. 'Surely you recognise Isabel?'

'Oh, Isabel,' said Mischa, in tones of satisfied relief. 'The last time I saw her she was sitting naked on a stone.' The giggles surprised him. He went on: 'By the swimming pool. I gave her a peppermint; I thought it might keep the flies away. But now of course she's different; she's changed a lot recently.'

And so there was a lively conversation, almost an argument. Everyone felt that Isabel had indeed changed; but how? And how uncanny that Mischa, so old and living apart, should have noticed.

Other people approached, and tactfully changed places. Old friends appeared as though by magic at his side, and one conversation slid into another, and even seemed to continue those begun many years before. There were no longer any gaps or tearings apart: only one continuous stream.

Food was brought. Plates on their knees, people caught Mischa's fork before it fell to the floor, wiped his mouth for him on the paper napkin, refilled his glass and put it between his frail fingers. His face was suffused with a beatific smile, as he made less and less effort to follow the words, remaining outside and yet the cause of all that went on.

There were so many people now, the room was quite full. Groups were forming and voices became bolder, deeper, richer in tone. The women, some of them beautiful, were subdued and quiet, the men a trifle more booming; but all was very decorous. A group at the table were talking about Mischa. 'But why after all shouldn't he do anything he likes? At his age – is it ninety-three? – no harm can come. And he still loves life. Swallow took him to the National Gallery the other day: but if he were to die looking at a Cézanne, wouldn't it be perfect?' Now it was put so clearly, with such common sense, all were agreed that Mischa had been free as air all his life and should not be hobbled or trammelled now. A delicate mechanism within him – something like the warning light that goes on when things get too hot – ensured his never getting stuck anywhere he did not want to be. One thing only counted, and that was painting; human beings were a game, an amusement, a play to be watched. If the actors thought, or made love, or quarrelled, it all took place on the other side of the footlights, while he looked on, often not understanding, but always fascinated. And sometimes he understood more than anyone realised, showing it by a shrewd remark or two which came as a shock to those who thought of him as merely a darling.

And so it was natural that the conversation was neither deep nor serious, and that there was a great deal of laughter on this, very likely his last, birthday party. Perhaps there is a proverb: gentle is as gentle does. It would have been suitable. And when Swallow wheeled him out to go to bed, it was almost as though a yogi were being carried shoulder-high through silent crowds saluting him for the last time.

When the morning came, he lay quietly awake, no need to be other than passive. Swallow arrived with coffee, later than usual, and found him extra lucid. 'Ethel is coming today, isn't she?' he said.

'Not Ethel, but Emily,' said Swallow, used to the mixing of generations.

'Oh yes, I mean Emily. When will she come?'

'This afternoon, I think,' said Swallow.

But when Emily arrived, who should have been but was not at the party, Mischa was speechless. Some slight infection had settled on his chest. He lay as before, hardly stouter than the stem of a plant under the quilt, with the canary, unused to company, fluttering here and there. Emily sat rather rigidly in the rocking chair, unable, for the wrong reasons, to make small talk. His hand was too frail for her to hold, his appearance too remote for risking a hug. Feeling it was for the last time, she wanted to elicit a response, but could only get as far as realising that her stare was too much like a burden for him, so she sat, allowing Swallow to talk, oddly, of the future and of death. She was there perhaps an hour. It was no use staying – she had a long way to go, and it seemed wrong that she was returning to the house in which Mischa had lived, and which would never see him again, while she would rattle about in it like a dried pea. A column of granite seemed to be growing inside her, blocking every outlet, preventing both move-ment and speech. She looked at him, and saw that he was already more than half on the other side. What was left was no more than a pressed leaf. She rose and bent over him and, to her shocked surprise, heard a small, clear voice, saying: 'Go home, my dear.' So she went.

The room, when Swallow left it, became quieter and quieter. It suggested a bubble about to burst and dissolve into a little patch of iridescent moisture. The tension held for a little longer, for a little longer the breathing continued. But when, in the evening, Swallow returned, it had ceased. There was nothing left, nothing, that is, that mattered.

Friendship

Helen remembered the first time she met them, four or five years ago. They called one Sunday, on impulse, at teatime. Carlotta, small and gentle, with a boy of about eleven, pale and extraordinarily beautiful, and Jonathan, tall, handsome and comparatively silent. They sat in a row on the sofa while Helen, delighted at the unexpectedness of the visit, served tea and mistakenly talked French. This was, she supposed, because of Carlotta's accent. When she got to know them better, she realised that Carlotta's mastery of English was more than adequate. The boy, Pierre, was interested by Helen's new compact disc player, and the parents – as she supposed they were – looked on with benign but unsentimental detachment. Helen was charmed by the boy's intelligence, by having been sought out so unexpectedly – a young couple, and apparently perceptive – and, after all the months of arid loneliness, that she had come across three people with whom she could exchange more, perhaps, than the commonplaces of ordinary intercourse.

This was not, in fact, the first time she had met them, since she had been given their address, though not their name, by a friend, when she was looking for someone to make her a model for a sculpture she was doing. She

231

remembered driving up to a barrack-like house, close to the road, but situated well above it, on a mound or hillock almost smothered with young plants. A large Great Dane, grey and brindled, approached her on ungainly legs from which hung huge, heavy paws. He barked once or twice, probably only for show, but Helen was relieved when Jonathan appeared to escort her to a cavernous workroom. On this occasion, too, the problem of language had arisen. From his dark colouring she had assumed Jonathan was French. But his command of the language suddenly appeared inadequate and, as her own French petered out, he said, in English, 'You're not French, are you?' and it turned out he was Australian.

But words did not come freely to either of them. As Helen was later to learn, Jonathan never talked easily, certainly not before he had reached a certain degree of intimacy, and even then his words came slowly, almost as though he found it difficult to get his tongue round them. Helen, preferring people who were not too brilliantly articulate, found this attractive. But it also made her feel as though she must tread delicately, as you might feel about a half-wild animal. Either there really was an aura of mystery round Jonathan, or she had created it which, even then, she had started filling with her own preferences. Sympathetic though he was, Jonathan had been neither reassuring nor encouraging. He appeared reluctant to do the work and yet he had accepted the job, and seemed to understand what she wanted with an ease Helen hadn't hoped for. But he had none of the down-to-earth quality of the typical craftsman. The second time she went to see him, doubt seized her: would he have produced anything at all? Perhaps she was confusing anxiety about her own artistic plans with doubt about his skill? In fact he had done exactly what she had asked for, and showed it to her modestly.

But the real beginning had been that Sunday when they dropped in for tea. Until then they had been shadowy, a piece of good luck rather than real people, partly because, being shy, it had not occurred to Helen to make friends. Still inhibited by the romance of living in France, by working there alone in isolation, she had failed to grasp the reality of individuals, of getting in touch, of having the courage to see what would happen. She had nearly foundered on depression, but had been saved by her doctor and, she was glad to say, by her own efforts. And she had produced enough work to have an exhibition in America, from where she had recently returned. At tea, she had showed photographs of her paintings to Jonathan and Carlotta, and their reaction had been positive, encouraging. She could not doubt their sincerity, and she had felt pleasantly like a sponge slowly filling with water.

It took her some time, she remembered, to become fully conscious of what they actually did. Their friendship seemed to her so delicate, even tenuous, she hated the idea of putting a foot wrong, although, as she thought of it now, she could not see how a direct question like that could have been taken amiss. And perhaps because of her lack of directness, there *had* been a moment of misunderstanding. She remembered Jonathan explaining that, even if he was compelled to use a camera, he was no ordinary photographer. And she experienced a feeling of privilege as he led her to a room up under the eaves, where his camera – ancient and square – stood on a table, its lens trained on to any object he placed beneath it. It had a solid, sensuous quality about it, and as Jonathan told her how it worked, she could see it had nothing to do with zoom lenses and swift enlargement or reduction. Helen felt reassured by his sensitivity to texture, much closer to a painter than a photographer in its sensuality. She was thrilled by his ability to transform, with his magic lantern, a piece of crinkled paper or a handful of dust into something monumental – for, once printed, his photographs were of immense size. What pleased her most was his rejection of colour in favour of the rich suggestiveness of black and white. In the work hanging on the walls she saw simplicity and classicism, qualities she responded to naturally, together with an underlying surrealism which connected it with modern life. It was a challenge, a quiet explosion – its beauty merely incidental.

It was through Carlotta and Jonathan that Helen came to know a gentle and lively man who was neither art dealer nor simply artist's friend, nor even connoisseur, but something of all three. Helen remembered the first of Carlotta's sculptures she had seen in Prosper's gallery in their local town. Each one sat on a pedestal in the centre, surrounded by the flotsam and jetsam of variable merit that Prosper had collected or been given during his long life. Helen's impression of the artwork was of something oddly at variance with what she knew of Carlotta's personality – elegant and delicate but also hard, brittle and transparent. It was not the elegance and delicacy that surprised her, but something uncompromising and determined, a quality that might have been singled out as fiercely intellectual. It took time, of course, for Helen to know what she felt. To start with her reaction had been vaguely unsympathetic, even defensive. Later she saw other works of this kind by Carlotta relegated to a corner of the studio, and she was thankful not to have to pronounce an opinion. She was conscious of a block of ice that stood in the way, not so much of liking or not liking, as of recognition. She felt at sea, and it was only after a long acquaintance with Carlotta, seeing her at home and with other people, as well as going with her to galleries and exhibitions, that an understanding of her work began to filter through.

They were soon visiting each other two or three times a week, each enchanted by the discovery of the other. Helen's loneliness dissolved like a mist in sunshine, sending her a little off balance. She overreacted, unable to prevent herself from producing lavish meals of cream, pastry and alcohol. Carlotta, with a smile, drew attention to this but, although Helen tried, she could not stop. Nor could she ever bring herself to say 'No' to an invitation, even if it threatened to interfere with her work. She was overwhelmed with the pleasure of novelty, of communication after a winter of silence; with the joy of watching youth and beauty, intelligence and humour.

And one evening as they sat by the fire, Helen said to Carlotta, 'You mustn't mind if I am silent. I am often shrouded by silence. It veils and envelops me and I am powerless to do anything about it.' Inside herself she said, Dear Carlotta, don't mind!

And she replied, 'Oh! But I do the same. I am shy and when I am with people I cannot get a word out. But with you I don't mind. I am quite happy.' So they smiled and were silent.

How delighted Helen was to feel herself accepted as an equal. At least thirty years older, old enough to be Jonathan's mother, Helen was only too conscious of her differences, not to say deficiencies – but they were swept aside unnoticed. There was also an enormous amount she did not understand. Jonathan's jokes sometimes left her floundering, only to be saved by Carlotta's ability to turn things deftly the right way out, giving them back their normal proportions. His jokes were surreal – he saw correspondences where Helen saw only incongruities, but when at last she understood, she was delighted. Pierre was quicker than she was, and would take up where Jonathan left off, amused to keep the shuttlecock flying. It took Helen time to realise that this partly sophisticated, partly juvenile humour was a protective device, improvised to stave off something more personal, more profound and serious.

One day they decided to go and see the gardens at La Mortola. Jonathan drove – he disliked being driven. Helen and Carlotta sat in a state of blissful irresponsibility as they drifted on winding roads, gazing at the rocky landscape against a dazzling blue sky and the variable green of the trees, both bright and, at times, almost black. One of their common interests was plants. Carlotta had an unerring eye for a rare plant growing by the roadside, and would cry out in excitement as she saw an aristolochia or a white saxifrage growing from a rocky cliff. Jonathan, equally excited, would stop the car and prise the plant from its bed in the stones, and take it home to join others they had found on previous expeditions.

When they eventually got to the garden rather late, there was no one else there. They wandered freely down its sloping paths and numerous flights of steps, overhung with the magnificent luxuriance of trees and shrubs, until at the bottom they found the sea lapping at their feet. They behaved like children – Helen was the worst – taking cuttings and popping them into plastic bags; even now Helen had an unidentified rose which had survived after one of these trips. The neglect of the garden seemed to add to its grandeur – the trees unpruned, the statues crumbling, the grass sprouting from broken steps, suggesting the protest of living creatures that, conscious of their past glory, grieved for their present misfortune. If they were an example of heart-breaking neglect, they were also one of magnificent survival. And then, Helen remembered, they unexpectedly came across an alley as neat as a newly swept carpet, decorated with pots of scarlet geraniums. They were all three horrified: they agreed about everything.

There were many other such expeditions, though now, at this distance, a little jumbled together in Helen's memory. Picnics in forests carpeted with anemones, an expedition far to the south to see specimens of styrax, a lunch with friends on a stony hillside where hundreds of Roman lamps had been found and where they found three large, blue-green lizards, peeping from gaps in the rocks.

And a small snake curled up on a stone. And a plant found by Carlotta, growing in a mulch of dead leaves and humus near the path. She took it home only to find, the following year, that it was a bunch of young beeches, an uncommon tree in that part of the world.

There were lunches too on the terrace of Jonathan and Carlotta's house, when Carlotta would produce delicious meals from nothing at all. Old Giles, an elderly English friend who was also an expert botanist, would sit there toying with his food and talking non-stop with an old-fashioned display of exquisite manners, spinning an atmosphere that was suave, well-oiled, intended to enchant and, because it came so naturally to him, succeeding. He hypnotised them all by his rarefied, mountain-air conception of life where conversation was its most highly-prized activity. Giles had built himself a house, coiled around a central staircase like a snailshell. Round it he had planted a whole forest of larch trees or fir trees of some sort, in whose shade grew hellebores and wild roses. Jonathan and Carlotta were fascinated by his wit and learning. To them he seemed exotic, detached and civilised – they visibly expanded in his presence, valuing him for his wide knowledge and his sense of humour. Helen, who had known many people not unlike him in England, was less tolerant – but even she had to admit that Giles had both authority and charm. She could see straight away that he was very attracted by Jonathan, which provoked a sort of amused tenderness in Carlotta while, although the attention made Jonathan a little shy, glanced off him hardly leaving a trace.

Helen had been thinking and remembering one morning, now after so many years, how Carlotta was with her son, Pierre. She had no doubt she loved him and gave much thought to him. But there was no warmth, no spontaneous affection, nothing physical, no touching – even no kindness, no forgiveness. More silence. Brown eyes with lids dropping over them. A sort of interminable waiting – for what? Helen remembered thinking. Were they always like this, even when she wasn't there? Carlotta had all the dignity of someone who withheld the most precious thing of all – whatever that might be. Yet while withholding it she also seemed to offer freedom. But what did Pierre want with such freedom, considering that, as soon as he said something, he was judged? Isn't it possible for a parent to give both warmth and freedom – or if not freedom, then the possibility of choice? It looked as though Carlotta had produced him, and then abandoned him to swim away on his own. Yes, seeing them together was like watching someone throw a baby in the water and then stand on the bank, waiting to see what would happen – never lifting a finger even when he started to

Friendship

go under. Helen did not think Carlotta was indifferent. But she would not help Pierre – or perhaps she could not? She refused to teach him or to take charge as a mother, and yet there was no one else to take her place. Oh! She was an odd mixture. Such a profound capacity for separating herself, for remaining apart and saying nothing – and then flaring at a touch like a firework, acting out a scene that had amused her, laughing until she forgot where she was. Sometimes she would recall an event when Pierre was a little boy and it was clear she had lived through it passionately. Silent though she often was, as though waiting for something, she was never impassive, never insensitive, never brutal. Unless you could call her coldness brutal? She reminded Helen of a faceted amber bead, reflective, glowing, which, to get the best from, you had to rub with a silk handkerchief.

Carlotta was against spoiling Pierre – no concessions were made because of his youth. He might drop with fatigue – in a restaurant, for example – but she would not go home until she was ready. All she could do was to look at him, not unkindly, not abrasively; but she saw his head dropping on his shoulder without apparent sympathy. They were *my* guests, Helen thought, how could I hurry them away? But her heart ached for Pierre. No doubt she was being sentimental – it was none of her business. But she could never resist saying something to

241

Pierre to give him a little encouragement. He would always react at once, smiling. It was like touching a sensitive plant, *Mimosa pudica*. And Carlotta's eyes continued to glow. Were they so close they did not need to show their feelings? Or could she really just be indifferent?

But Carlotta gave nothing away. She committed none of the ordinary mistakes of mothers who are conscious of their children's criticism, who have lost touch to the point of pleading for understanding, almost bribing for love. No unnecessary endearments, in fact nothing unnecessary almost to the point of lack of tenderness, to the point of realising that we lived in a different climate. Helen understood that Carlotta refused to manipulate – that is what it amounted to. No doubt it was hard to do, but she never got the impression that Carlotta pretended – ever. It must have been hard for Pierre, but he had been brought up with it after all. He had never had too many toys, he had never been corrupted. From the beginning he had been treated as an adult, that is as someone who mattered, someone whose strength was always equal to the occasion. But he had been deprived of his childhood, brought up in a world where there was a chilling lack of reciprocity and where, although the love was sure and honest, it was never expressed.

Helen never doubted Carlotta's love for Pierre until one day when Pierre was at school and Jonathan and Carlotta had come over for supper, along with Helen's daughter

Nel. They discussed Pierre's future, the rather awful school he was at, and indulged in dreams of a better one. Carlotta remained realistic throughout the conversation, doubtful of changes for the better. Afterwards Nel pronounced passionately that Pierre was unloved! And as she was a most loving creature, Helen was stopped in her tracks, and made to think.

Of course Pierre had the usual problems of most boys of fifteen: he was intelligent – perhaps *very* intelligent – and yet his school-work was poor. He was neither entirely at home in English or in French. His masters were indifferent, cold and unfriendly, and he had no friends; he was lonely. He both lied and cheated in self-defence. Every week he came home from school on a bus that took two hours, and when his mother was away friends sometimes took him in. He always seemed a little lost and vaguely unhappy, and yet he was still responsive, making plenty of jokes. He was vulnerable – all the more so because of his near angelic beauty. And in spite of her apparent indifference, Carlotta worried about him. She hated his problems, but she never considered that maybe love and affection might be the answer; nor did she ever try to teach him, but watched him flounder without her.

There was something admirable about her behaviour, Helen thought. She was certainly not one of those mothers who constantly prompt their children to behave in a certain way; she let him get on with it, which in some ways he did very well. Yet when he was not there she complained of his behaviour, despite the fact that socially he had excellent manners. Once on a walk, when he was staying the weekend alone with Helen, they explored a little valley together, where the orchids grow and the bee-eaters nest. At the upper end, the stream, meagre enough, meanders between shaly hillocks and the landscape becomes more and more lunar, tempting one to climb still further and see what happens beyond. Pierre was the leader of the expedition, giving Helen his hand at every difficult crossing, hauling her up steep slopes like the hero in a fairy tale. He was full of grace and charm, as delicate as the most sophisticated man about town, although he was still largely a child. He spent most of the Saturday in his room working, and in the evening he showed Helen the results of some small, interim exams – she was shocked at the low standard of his answers. The endings of the French verbs defeated him, and the geography exam was a vague trail of red chalk wandering across the paper. Pierre explained to her what his school was like – she was horrified at the barrack-like aridity, the lack of human warmth and welcome; the environment completely devoid of beauty.

It was the combination of beauty, grace – undoubtedly inherited from Carlotta – and liveliness that made Pierre an exceptional boy. Having been brought up as an adult he was, though immature, never childish. Quick-witted, he was well able to hold his own in the rather ironic, sophisticated conversation that carried on around him. He contributed a lot to each social event, leavening the atmosphere with his humour and lightness. He was extraordinarily detached about himself, his experience and the role he expected to play in life. This too was an attitude encouraged by his education. If he had an axe to grind, it was being sharpened in secret.

Carlotta allowed him space in which to breathe, and never told him what to say. But she accepted his contributions very coolly, and only opened her mouth to find fault or to criticise. Sometimes, stammering in an endeavour to hold his own, he would try to justify his opinion; but he seldom succeeded. Carlotta's manner was formal, dismissive. And he accepted it gracefully, as he did everything. Only on a very few occasions was there anything approaching a 'scene' and usually for some very minor infringement of normal behaviour, such as not wanting to go to bed so early. This was indeed childish, but to Helen's mind, so understandable!

Helen was shocked. In her own experience school had been inefficient and confusing. It hadn't really helped her to live any better, but nor had it been a totally negative experience, since the place, a Georgian house in the drab lands of Essex, had been beautiful and this, she now saw, had been tremendously important. There had also been friendships, rather nebulous, but reflecting her own inclinations at the time. And there had been an art teacher whom she definitely would have given a lot to please. What riches and opportunity compared to Pierre's experiences! His answers to Helen's questions revealed an atmosphere more like that of a prison than a school. Pierre said nothing about his fellow pupils. Friends were, apparently, the last sort of thing he expected to find. There was one master who counted for something with him, one person who showed a glimmer of affection. Even he, however, went only so far with his pupil, showing insufficient concern for his lack of progress. But Pierre felt nothing like self-pity – he accepted what seemed to him the inevitable, with precocious detachment and even a sense of humour. In fact his humour was very like Jonathan's – an imitation as Helen supposed – and seemed to come to him very naturally. Helen could see that it was a form of self-protection against future consequences, and she could not help wondering what Jonathan and Pierre were afraid of.

As male members of the family, were they afraid of going deeper? Admittedly both were intelligent, and she could see that they succumbed to the temptation of being funny, bright and quick – seeing the bizarre in life and earning a quick laugh – being successful without paying for it. That she herself always fell for this and enjoyed it was, to a certain extent, proof of its efficacy. It was difficult to remain calm and ask further questions which might suddenly seem too serious. Sometimes Helen could stem the tide, but found it more difficult with Pierre because underneath this effervescence there was a sadness that prompted her to feel that gaiety of any kind was tremendously welcome.

At his school there was nothing aesthetic – no art, no music and, if there was any literature, its thrills and beauties were overlaid by the French habit, which Helen sometimes felt could be called a passion, for the *idée reçue*, so derided by Flaubert. Pierre could only escape the doldrums by dreaming – and his dreams were powerful, sweeping him into a world of fantasy that compensated for his disappointments. On their walk that weekend, Helen was impressed by his sense of style, inspired by a longing to weigh anchor and mount upwards in a gas balloon. He had imagined or 'invented' a tiny, one-man aeroplane that could be transformed into a car and in which he proposed to make huge hops, like a grasshopper, about the countryside, always arriving at the moment anything interesting was going on. He didn't say he wished to be the Batman hero, sweeping in to guarantee the happy ending, and in this proved himself superior to most children. There was something in his thinking that suggested a certain fatalism that precluded all such things as happy endings and, Helen sometimes feared, happiness *tout court.*

Two or three years earlier, before Helen had been there to offer Pierre a home for the occasional weekend, Carlotta had sometimes arranged for him to stay with her English friends at La Blache – a village they had bought up entirely, and rebuilt for summer visits of large groups of friends from London. There is no doubt Pierre's beauty and brightness had been his attraction, and he had been spoiled by the gilded and pampered youth that had flooded in from the north. All they wanted was to enjoy themselves for a few weeks in a place that suggested all the delicious artificiality and freedom of the island of Cythera. It was spectacularly beautiful, enjoying a view bathed in the clear, azure air of the south. No undesirable person came near them. They were a law and a world unto themselves, and impregnated Pierre's young mind with a conception of life that had nothing to do with the everyday or the normal. It was, in a sense, manna from heaven, but was insidiously poisoned with the idea that if you had enough money, this was the most desirable kind of existence.

Spending weeks at a time there without the ballast of Carlotta's common sense or the masculine, if somewhat cool presence of Jonathan, Pierre responded to being

spoiled – something that never happened to him at home
– and no doubt mistook a light-hearted affection for something more long-lasting and real. Helen, who had not
been a witness to all this, could only take it from Carlotta
that Pierre had been seduced and had lost his head and
heart at the same time. Wanting to help, but fearful of
stepping beyond the limits of true friendship, Helen had
the idea of finding – and paying for – another, more
humane school. But before she had decided how and when
to intervene, things had taken their own course. Pierre's
school complained of his behaviour and Carlotta sent him
to another one a little nearer home.

Helen remembered a conversation with Carlotta when
they were all at dinner together, when she had talked
about her life in America, fraught with problems about
Pierre and her first husband. She said she had seen every
psychiatrist in the city and had found none of them
helpful, indeed barely satisfactory. She knew all the psychological ropes, and had found them wanting. And yet at
the time she was mystified by Pierre's behaviour. He was,
Helen thought, simply feeling frustrated and misunderstood, even unloved, like so many of the young, either
with or without reason – that was where Helen felt unsure.
Sometimes she saw Carlotta's behaviour with him as amazingly cold and unsympathetic, while at other moments
she found herself admiring this detachment, believing that

this quality actually signified a love that went deeper than the usual signs of affection. Now, however, Carlotta, in common with many other mothers, could not read the true meaning behind his intermittent gestures of adolescent despair, and began telling him how to behave, and what not to do – all the oughts and shoulds that, as far as her own behaviour went, she seemed so well able to regard with humorous disbelief and scepticism.

Nevertheless it was also Carlotta who brought the situation back to *terra firma*. But her interventions – excellent in intention – did not always have the desired effect. Helen could not say that Jonathan was insensitive; but he was too witty, too amusing, forcing Carlotta to be over-serious. And then Pierre would be silent and withdraw from this contest he wanted nothing to do with. A shadow enveloped him. Was it, Helen wondered long afterwards, jealousy – or rather envy of the evident closeness that existed between his mother and Jonathan, who was not, as Helen had originally supposed, Pierre's father.

Carlotta had met Pierre's father in Italy. She had run away from her home in France; Helen did not know why her home was so bad. There was a mother, but she never heard tell of a father. Carlotta had a nervous breakdown, from which she finally rescued herself by running away – or this is what Helen understood had happened. She did not of course tell her all this at once, but Helen pictured her living in a French village alone with her mother. So after a few sessions with a psychiatrist, she ran away, maybe with a lover – maybe not. She was a wild girl, and did a little of everything, finally arriving on the Italian border where she was picked up by a man in a smart sports car, who said he would take her to Rome. They stopped in a filling station where the radio was on. There was an urgent call for a white sports car and its owner who had, it reported, stolen a lot of jewellery. She had listened calmly, and so did the man in the garage. There was the sports car in front of them with its number plate and probably the jewellery somewhere inside it – but neither of them did anything about it. Carlotta got in again and was taken to Rome, deposited in the Piazza del Popolo. He took her to have a drink and left her in the café with the bill to pay – taking her suitcase with him.

Carlotta didn't know anyone in Rome – and Helen never heard how she found her saviour, a family man – a charmer and cultivated. He took her to live with him and his family, and she got a job, started everything anew. Always, when Rome was referred to, she remembered her life there with nostalgia.

One year Carlotta went to Sicily on holiday. She loved it there since she could live on practically nothing at all, and get taken out to sea by the fishermen, returning at dawn with a boatful of fish caught by torchlight. It was there she met a young American, a type of person with whom she was unfamiliar. He was young, amusing and – to judge from the beauty of his son – good-looking. He took her back to Utah and married her. It was as though she had been swallowed by both Jonah and the whale: her parents-in-law were Mormons and horribly strict – and her husband also a Mormon, turned out to be a drug addict.

A child was born and, within the year, Carlotta decided she could bear it no longer. The husband's family decided Carlotta was no good as a mother and took Pierre away from her. And once again she ran away, this time to San Francisco. But she wanted her son. Having no money, she took a Greyhound bus back to Utah, stole her son, and returned to San Francisco. She must have had some kind of success there because by the time Jonathan arrived, she had a business and property.

When Helen first got to know them, Jonathan and Carlotta seemed a very united couple, and this charmed her. They understood each other as though by private telepathy, especially about questions of art, not needing to say more than a word or two to know what the other thought. Helen listened delighted, but quite often felt out of her depth. She wasn't in touch with modern American art and she instinctively reacted against it. She found it hard and inhuman, over-intellectual and unrelated to anything she liked. If she didn't exactly hide her feelings, she remained silent, hoping greater knowledge would help her to change her mind. She was left feeling old, and rather out of it. It took her a little time to realise that neither Carlotta nor Jonathan had much knowledge of painting. They were historically ignorant, which at first shocked her. But they disarmed her too, saying they were aware of their lack of education – that neither of them would know how to paint if given the chance, and Helen began to understand how different their attitude was from hers. She saw, briefly, what it had been like in America for them, and envied them their freedom from excessive education. Nothing worried them: they reacted to anything they found stimulating with a mixture of humour and sensibility, free from the sort of pretension that dogged her own footsteps.

They had decorated their house in a style very different from Helen's own which, by comparison, was colourful, but slapdash. Mostly all white, since that was Carlotta's preference, their house was beautifully finished and elegant. They never spent money unnecessarily, they never splashed out but instead, facing temptation, became reflective and critical. Often Helen thought they were on the verge of buying a book, a knife, a silver teaspoon – but in the end they didn't, mostly, she thought, because Carlotta's sense of reality restrained them. Helen would feel rather gross because she could afford to buy something even when she was unsure of how much she liked it. And she gave them things occasionally, thus acquiring, she hoped, goodwill – even affection

It was only after a while that she began to see that their relationship was not as good either as it had once been, or as she had hoped it was. Oddly enough it was Carlotta who seemed to have the thinner skin of the two. It was obvious that she dominated practical life. Perhaps it was her French blood. She was, on the whole, tactful with her suggestions, but, Helen thought, it may even have been this that rather irritated Jonathan. He would complain if he thought that too much was being asked of him, but would usually comply in the end. Sometimes, however, he would raise his head and reproach Carlotta with some forgetfulness, or simply for doing things differently from the way he would have done them himself. And in response she would complain, part fretfully and part irritatedly, and underneath her complaint Helen would feel a much deeper layer of distress, something that irked her profoundly, which she could neither identify nor bring out into the open. There was a lot of pain there, lying in an unholy muddle at the bottom of Carlotta's psyche.

One beautiful day in September the three of them went off in the car to see an exhibition, or maybe it had simply been for fun – for the pleasure of an outing and to see new places and unknown faces. They had stopped in Uzès, as Helen remembered, a town where Gide spent much of his youth – she enjoyed connections of this kind – and lunched in a small but good restaurant in the middle of the town. They felt happy and close. It was not too long after the beginning of their friendship and in the course of conversation Helen found herself a little embarrassed, not knowing whether to allude to them as a married couple, or not. She thought they were probably a couple without the marriage. But they laughed and said, 'Oh! But actually, we *are* married!' It was a huge joke; and they went on to describe their marriage ceremony in America – all its ludicrous aspects emphasised, the unconventionality and even frivolity. Even Pierre had been there too. According to Jonathan it had been a hole-and-corner affair, rapid and hardly attended by anyone else.

As Helen listened to their jokes and witnessed how much pleasure it gave them to recall that occasion, she got a much clearer idea of the nature of their relationship, which Carlotta afterwards had told her was very intense for the first few years. Pierre had been but a baby, carted round in a soap-box and sometimes left in charge of the Great Dane belonging to Carlotta. He was not forgotten or, as it might seem, neglected. He simply grew up in the shade of two people who were enthralled by each other, and saw life more wittily and less conventionally than other people. Pierre had even profited from such an education: a certain freedom had been offered to him from the start without the stress of the oughts and shoulds that burden so many other children. Carlotta required him to be as adult as possible, and he responded gallantly. Helen only wondered whether there wasn't something missing, the lack of which had somehow turned him into a sort of Pierrot Lunaire, searching for the key that would reverse the process.

Helen realised that her relationship with both Jonathan and Carlotta centred round the fact that they were artists. At first this may have been only a snobbish, superficial feeling, but the fact remained that it was through their art that they found a way into her life. It gave them an extra dimension as well as being a subject they all three felt deeply about. Helen envied them for being a couple, for having a common pursuit and purpose, for carrying within them a flame, a seriousness that nourished them. Like a couple of birds sitting on a cliff, they had flown and might fly again, and Helen wanted to fly with them. At least thirty years older than they were, she had never grown wings and even now hardly hoped to.

There was no harm, she realised, in her falling a little in love with Jonathan – something which on his side he did not completely reject. But there was no reality in it. It was 'love' in inverted commas and the weakness made her almost ashamed – an enormous, irresistible temptation which she knew she should have avoided. It gave her great pleasure, and even gave a meaning to her otherwise too solitary life. It was not as though such a feeling could harm Carlotta – it was too unreal – and perhaps this was its chief charm, since it meant that she could be selfish without self-reproach, pretend she was on the same wavelength as him in both life and art, and could ignore those things that didn't work. She may have seemed like a bloodsucker, a vampire – the image pursued her – but she turned a blind eye to it. She remembered the afternoon she realised she was in love. She had been alone, waiting for Jonathan to come and help her plant some trees. Carlotta had been away for a few days, and Helen had asked him over, offering him a meal in exchange for an afternoon's work. Why not? she thought. A lonely, elderly woman needs a young man's help. She did not admit to herself it was a lure, it was carrying on in the way her family had always behaved, without realising everything that lay beneath such behaviour. She was a spoiled child, justified in having what she wanted. At that moment a little more insight might have helped her to see clearly –

but instead, looking out at the distant hills, she made the unreal promise to herself that she would not, come what may, fall in love seriously, she would only enjoy Jonathan's friendship – a promise easily made and forgotten as soon as Jonathan appeared. He was generous and the afternoon agreeable. But she had the sense to realise that it was a one-off occasion, not to be repeated – he made it clear that whether she planted trees or not was her own affair.

Helen saw that Jonathan's attitude, while full of genuine modesty, was a distinguished one. He was aristocratic, and in control of his own destiny. Had she said so, he would have laughed at her, almost self-consciously blushing. But he would have known it was true. He greatly needed and often asked for Carlotta's support. True, they did not stay together for nothing, however precarious their relationship. But the things he saw – that is, his personal vision which came to light in his photographs rose from depths that were hidden even from himself. Did he remind her of a bear, floundering in a forest? At any rate it was evident that he lived in a dream, providentially fertile, and protected by a facility for making jokes. Sometimes, however, he could be tricked into talking seriously about his intentions, his hopes and his ideas. It was as though not the bear but the leopard had paid her the compliment of sitting on her knee – but only for five minutes – and then only if she really listened, she really wanted to understand. These were moments Helen cherished, and which contributed greatly to her feelings for Jonathan without, it seemed, arousing any shade of jealousy in Carlotta.

Jonathan also had exhibitions – what else had they to live on? Not that exhibitions are a way of earning money – and certainly his were not – but there is always a hope that one day an explosion will take place, and the dollars come rolling in. Naturally both Jonathan and Carlotta were fatalistically sceptical about the possibility of such success, but they were ambitious, not so much for money as for appreciation, and exhibitions were therefore events of prime importance. Exhibitions largely happened abroad, and after one in Germany where he had won a prize, Carlotta came back with stories of having been disgracefully treated by their hosts who evidently had no idea of how penniless or how proud they were. Refusing the insensitivity and arrogance with which they were treated, they found themselves walking the streets for hours with nothing in their stomachs, only to end up, fortunately, in the apartment of a more imaginative friend. Helen was not told much about the exhibition itself – whether from real modesty or forgetfulness, she was not sure.

Helen did see one exhibition, however, in La Charité, at Marseille, the magnificent building once dedicated to the poor and destitute, now transformed into a centre of art where the architecture is based on the classical qualities of simplicity and coolness, enclosing an immense space of airy splendour in which one might see anything from Giacometti to Tinguely. Jonathan's photographs were large, black and white and impressive; they circled round a single idea and were all of the same size, hung in a row against the pale walls.

Jonathan's vulnerability was as apparent as an opencast mine, barely hidden by his sense of the bizarre – a quality that made him, in Helen's eyes at least, so attractive. Carlotta, in one of her more extraordinary analyses, said he was incapable of thinking, that this was a process that never took place in his handsome, Pompeian head, with its expression of gentle, ironic humour. But Helen found this statement grotesquely exaggerated. She saw a lot of thought in what he did – not cerebral thought, but feeling thought, if one can so define it, which was born not simply of a desire for success but from a poetic vision and a need to understand and comment on the world. Jonathan's thought processes came of the combustion that seized him when he suddenly saw something unusual, beyond the normally visible. Carlotta's thinking was never of this sort. She was French after all and had the typically Gallic gift for words, for creating convincing if ephemeral temples in the air of intellectual excitement.

*   *   *

Things seemed to be going well and yet they had no money. Since Jonathan expressed himself almost entirely in asides, it often took Helen quite a while to understand what was going on. She couldn't really remember how it happened that, when it became apparent that he hadn't enough money to work for the exhibition in Germany, she gave him a cheque – not a fortune but enough for him to realise his ambitions for the event. The exhibition was a success and she had sufficient faith in his star to talk of repayment in the future and to hope that, without undue strain, he would be able to give her back what she had lent him. No doubt there was a certain vanity in her act. She was posing as a Maecenas, a tradition to which, in some rather vague way, she wanted to belong.

It was important not to forget that Carlotta was also an artist. Some time after Jonathan's show Helen suggested Carlotta should have an exhibition in the field outside her house. It was an ideal situation, a remote but accessible farmhouse in a wild valley without a village in sight, overlooked by a mountain more than a thousand metres high. Hard rocks covered only by sheep-nibbled turf formed the barren but tree-clothed slopes of the hills, while at the bottom of her small piece of land were four or five splendid oaks, harbouring hoopoes and golden orioles. Helen presented the idea to Carlotta with some tact along with her enthusiasm, and she consented to have a show in August – the best month for such an undertaking.

Helen was pleased, even thrilled, but also had a niggling feeling of doubt that she could not explain. These were uncharted, grey areas. Wasn't an exhibition like this the sort of thing you could only do if you had unqualified enthusiasm for the artwork? If someone had asked Helen whether she took this trouble because she so much admired Carlotta's work, what would she reply? If she had said that, more than admiration, it was a desire to help, didn't this sound immensely patronising? Wasn't she putting herself into a false position? And, if she was honest with herself, she knew that she lacked a sense of security: if she couldn't achieve success herself, she would do so on the back of somebody else. She had only one, very lame answer: her personal opinion of Carlotta's work was irrelevant. A week or so before the show Carlotta and Jonathan paced the ground, plotting locations for pieces of wood and cardboard, metal and bright blue paint, and leaving Helen to look on with her nose a trifle out of joint. Then invitation cards were printed, and they had a shopping day in Aix when, on impulse, Helen bought Carlotta a white dress with a full skirt and a low neckline which metamorphosed her into a prima ballerina. Her round, heavy-lidded eyes glowed – she resembled a Victorian print of Taglioni.

Friendship

All was set for an open day in the sun-baked, arid month of August and, as they waited for the first arrivals, it started to rain. It reminded Helen of that moment at the opera when someone announces that the principal singer is to be replaced by another. But perhaps it was a sign that softness and gentleness would grace the occasion. Carlotta, Helen and one or two others retreated into the salon, a large, vaulted room previously used for sheep, and sat there telling anecdotes about Giono, a French writer whose haunts were not far away. Eventually the rain stopped, and people began to arrive in far larger quantities than they had expected.

Helen was the hostess, but was unknown to all except the elderly guests, who tended to sink into deckchairs or sit on low walls with a glass of the mildly alcoholic drink she had provided. Hordes of English friends appeared like swallows, and filled the field with chatter and laughter. Carlotta disappeared among them and Helen hoped they were genuinely interested – they had, several of them, reputations as art lovers. The hordes soon departed, and the friends sat under the lime tree to drink and listen to the reminiscences of a Greek gentleman who had somehow been left behind. He got into an argument with Jonathan about something totally abstract and rather boring, and Helen suddenly realised that Jonathan was drunk. How he had managed it on the concoction she had made she could barely imagine. But it was evident that for him something, perhaps everything, was wrong, that he was seeing nothing as everyone else saw it. He was having a nightmare. Yet even when Jonathan became obstreperous Carlotta sat dignified and quiet, taking no notice. When finally they and all the stragglers had gone, Helen was left with a feeling of a job done as well as possible; yet no sales to show for it. They had shot their arrow – but had not hit the bull's eye.

It cannot have been very long after this – perhaps in the following year – that Helen proposed she and Carlotta take a holiday in England. They would drive there in Helen's car and she would pay all the expenses. Full of curiosity to see how her English friends lived, Carlotta could hardly refuse such a good offer.

They had just set off and, as they entered the approach to the motorway, a car ran into them. A woman got out of the other car and said, as they assessed the damage: 'It's all my fault. It's the third time I've done exactly the same thing.' The boot of the car was jammed and their necks were stiff for a week afterwards; but they continued on their journey.

Carlotta did not often drive, mainly because Jonathan wanted always to do so and even when the three of them went out in Helen's car it was usually he who drove –

Helen having learned that it was the only way he could be happy. He drove well, if a little inclined to shoot the amber unnecessarily. Since she had lived in America for such a long time, Carlotta was forced to get a new driving licence, and had passed the exam without a single mistake, coming first in a batch of fellow applicants. So on this trip she shared the driving with Helen.

It rained. The drops bounced off the blue-black asphalt and streamed down the windscreen in blinding torrents. Although Carlotta drove ahead with confidence, she tired sooner than Helen whose energy lasted longer. They spent two nights in hotels of an ordinary and modest description. It was a change from their normal lives, and as such very welcome. Yet Helen was aware of a certain feeling of restraint, a disappointing lack of intimacy which may have been the effect of fatigue or the feeling that Carlotta had let herself in for an adventure over which she had no control. Nevertheless, Helen did her utmost to put Carlotta's needs first.

The sea, if not actually rough, was choppy and made Carlotta feel ill. They sat in a claustrophobic lounge, spiritually anathema to both of them, but Helen, familiar with such discomfort, had taken a pill for seasickness. Carlotta, however, feared the effect of pills, and the nearer they came to Dover felt worse and worse. By the time they arrived she looked green and exhausted, and Helen, anticipating the fatigue of the journey into London, searched for another solution. Another hotel? No: so she found herself ringing the bell of a friend's house – friends she didn't know any too well but who were fellow painters. They were the perfect rescuers, the perfect hosts, and gave them wine and spaghetti for supper. Their house, moreover, was a delight in itself – a strange, rich and rare mixture of oddities.

The following morning they set out for London, arriving in the huge and monstrous metropolis at about lunch time. They were intrigued by the flat they had been loaned on the south side of the river, in Battersea. There was ample room for two but they both slowly came to feel that it was congested with objects that had no meaning even to their owner – it was like a squirrel's nest. Collected with enthusiasm, these things were now evidence of failure and despair, as they silted up the blind spaces, producing an overwhelmingly depressing atmosphere.

Helen, of course, had her own reasons for being in England and on occasion left Carlotta alone. But she never came back to the flat to find Carlotta had enjoyed herself, or that she had been anywhere interesting. Where were these friends who were going to help her? What exactly was she looking for, where was the little flame that would spring into a bigger blaze and warm her, making her forget her disappointments and her loneliness? As Helen remembered it, the only result of her effort to be a good friend to Carlotta was failure and pain. She did not know what was wrong – but perhaps the greatest mistake of all, Helen thought, was to worry about it.

Whether from stupidity or insensitivity, Helen continued to try to help. When they got home again her three daughters, Anne, Mary and Nel, came to stay. They were between forty and forty-five, gifted and beautiful – but, she had to admit, extraordinarily immature. One evening they were all invited to supper with Jonathan and Carlotta. The table, newly painted, was lit by candlelight, the plates were probably bought at the flea market and each a different colour, and the atmosphere was expectant and delightful. Jonathan was on his best behaviour, even paying heed to social conventions and making fewer jokes than usual.

But Helen's daughters were not impressed. They refused to surrender to their hosts' evident desire to please. First one daughter could not eat what was put in front of her and called for an omelette, and when another couldn't stop talking, Helen sat by transfixed with embarrassment. They left, and she drove home in silence, ashamed, and – yet worse – ashamed of being ashamed. Were her children – and she herself, for that matter – so arrogant? It was a reproach that had always been levelled at her family, an accusation she hoped she had vanquished – but here it was again, growing, unobserved and malevolent. Jonathan and Carlotta said nothing about her daughters. Whatever they felt was absorbed into an immediate past that was rapidly becoming, for Helen, more and more laden with a mixture of strange feelings. When her daughters went away she was left on her own again to live a life, if not as solitary as it had been, still concentrated almost wholly on herself. Her painting seemed blocked. She envied Jonathan and Carlotta their professionalism and their detachment. In this they seemed to understand each other perfectly and shared a confidence in their own vision, which made them indifferent to artistic or worldly success. They seemed to Helen very pure – whereas somehow she was not – and she could not make out why.

Although the supper party had left behind it a sense of failure, Helen had nonetheless seen Carlotta and Nel lost for an instant in a private, secret embrace. They seemed to enjoy an understanding more natural and spontaneous than anything Helen herself felt for Carlotta, or Carlotta for Helen. Her admiration, genuine though it was, got her nowhere. She longed for love much too desperately, but had not received a single sign from Jonathan. It took a long time for Helen to realise the hopelessness of her position; so for the moment she hung on, still acting the part of Maecenas and benefactor. And it was in this role that she bought two of Jonathan's photographs, several feet square and difficult to accommodate in a house with little wall space. Their black and white shapes appealed to her sense of austerity; her sense of the abstract was acute – she was less sensitive to the purely human, the small and the touching.

One day Jonathan rang Helen with the news that their friend Prosper had been brutally murdered in his own house. A knife had been stuck between his shoulder blades while his back was turned. No one knew who the murderer was, although one or two people were suspected and questioned. It was only after several months that the criminal was found to be a wretched fellow who had murdered for the sake of three or four hundred francs left on the writing table. This only made the tragedy worse.

They had seen their friend Prosper quite often. He came from a well-known local family and was much loved and respected in their small town. He had, Helen realised, been a great help to Jonathan and Carlotta when they had first come over from America. He had occupied a unique position in local society, being the only person who had a natural taste for art and literature yet was neither pretentious nor self-conscious. He had enjoyed life; careless of convention, he used to walk about town in his slippers as though he were in his own kitchen. The traffic stopped for him, and everyone smiled at his harmless eccentricities. He had been very hospitable and his apartment, right in the middle of the town, had been full of interesting art, some of it by Jonathan and some by Carlotta. He had cared little for money and, in the habit of leaving his front door open, had been robbed of all he possessed more than once. But he had survived these misfortunes and continued to be important to the town, managing a gallery where he had put on frequent and interesting exhibitions. Helen went to them, got to know him and both liked and respected him. He was on excellent terms with both the local artists and the town administration yet had no vested interests nor longing for power. He cultivated his garden quietly, and wished for nothing else.

Both Jonathan and Carlotta were extremely upset at the news of his death. They were shaken – particularly Carlotta – and they came to share their distress with Helen. All three sat round the stove going over the little they knew of the circumstances, so horrible and shocking. Crime – the word that belonged to cheap newspapers and scandal-mongering magazines – had entered their lives by a back door, and had blindly, for no reason at all, deprived them of a loved and valued friend.

As time went by Helen worried about her relationship with Jonathan and Carlotta. There were many things she still did not understand – and yet nothing she could really put her finger on, nothing that could account for her feelings of guilt. Her love for Jonathan, or rather the nature of his attraction for her, she had succumbed to, perfectly aware of its unreality. This very unreality made her love seem forgivable, while at the same time she knew it was wrong, and blamed herself for it. Her feelings for Carlotta were far more down to earth, and, perhaps oddly, more intense. Carlotta was not a beauty, but Helen loved looking at her – her round, dark, hooded eyes, her small head and her expression of detached, often slightly sad or wry amusement. Her usual manner was calm and relaxed, she took time to do things, and did them with elegance and precision. She imparted a flavour of her own to everything she did, giving the impression that she neither wished nor asked for anyone else's approval. Her dignity enveloped and protected her, investing her with an unconscious authority that Helen envied, since she was unable to cash a cheque at the bank without saying 'thank you' ten times over.

The more time they spent together the more Helen came to see the profound differences that existed between them. One of the things that most delighted her about Jonathan was his way of calling attention to unusual and bizarre accidents of appearance – things nobody else would have noticed but which his sense of the ridiculous transformed into something they could all laugh at. Helen was blind to these subtleties; but for Jonathan it was natural. He illuminated the world as though he had a box of matches in his pocket: Carlotta took Jonathan's outbursts very much in her stride, and sometimes added her own view of the world the right way up. Helen realised that she never saw things for themselves – for her it was the whole that was important, the relation of each thing to the other rather than their intrinsic individuality. Her pyjamas were blue, but they were only that particular blue because of the red next to them. But she came to see that Jonathan and Carlotta were far more intrigued by the personality of each thing. They saw things Helen didn't and even couldn't see. Jonathan's way of seeing was that of a scientist with a sense of humour whereas Carlotta's was more emotional, more poetic, a point of view that, to some extent, Helen shared. Yet while Helen felt that plants were living creatures and loved the drudgery of gardening, Carlotta's way with plants was more sensitive, her handling more delicate. She gave the plant the space it needed. Jonathan was ready to climb any crag or mountain to winkle a plant from its crevice, but once it was planted in the garden he tended to lose interest. When it died he would simply shrug his shoulders and made a joke at his own expense. It was an intelligent way of asking for forgiveness – and what could they do but smile?

Helen had no difficulty in seeing the intimate connection between Jonathan and his work. His images, however abstract, were in some indirect but felicitous way self-portraits. What he couldn't put into words came out clearly in his photographs. But the apparent gulf between Carlotta's sculpture and drawings and her own personality struck Helen dumb. It produced in her a state of non-comprehension that overcame her desire to sympathise, putting her in a false position from which, alas, she hadn't the courage to extricate herself. Helen could remember one occasion at her house when Carlotta talked at length about her artistic development, her feelings as to what, for her, was most worthwhile. She was, of course, a post-modernist who had come to maturity in America, and for whom this new art presented no problems. Her inclinations were largely political and she had evidently given a lot of thought to the important questions, but she was not a woman of theory and she had no desire to impose her ideas on others. Helen was ashamed to realise that she had never thought of art in this way. When they went to exhibitions together she pointed things out to her, helping her to understand not only the work itself but the ideas that lay behind it, introducing Helen to a new concept of art which reconnected it with life. But where were these qualities in Carlotta's own work? True, she had obviously had a moment of vision once – but it had failed and got stuck. Her work, so luminous and spirited in intent, seemed to have become all the things Carlotta herself was not – hard, aggressive and monotonous, with gates like teeth or slits that resembled letter boxes. Did she feel she was imprisoned, or was she longing for a correspondent? After all these years, Helen realised that had she recognised something of this kind then, she might have been able to help her.

At Nîmes they saw an exhibition Helen knew she would never forget, and she would never have seen without Carlotta and Jonathan. It was in a commercial gallery in an ancient grain-store building. The artist was an American, compelled to call his work sculpture because there was no other word for it, but it was made of things so ephemeral, so lacking in seriousness and so delightful that Helen was entranced – blown off her feet. Unlike anything else she had ever seen these sculptures seemed to confirm something she already knew, and had known for a long time. The exhibits were three-dimensional, composed of all manner of things, from feathers to tin or plastic, and dripping with colour. Bunches of beads were fastened to the wall with sellotape, others were hung on flimsy pedestals, every niche and corner was filled.

Space was created out of nothing, and yet it was almost tangible. Helen was enchanted – a door had been opened for her, a glimpse of new possibilities, shining and tempting. She went home in a state of euphoria.

From that day on Helen knew her life had been changed. She began hunting for old bits of iron, for plastic, glass, wood or string, anything she could glue, cut, saw or paint. She was possessed by a feverish excitement and communicated it to Jonathan and Carlotta – perhaps mostly to Carlotta, who helped her with thoughtful criticism and advice, knowing where to find things and how to put them together. At first Helen was too ambitious – she was still thinking of Michelangelo. But as she created she learned new ways of looking and seeing – even new ways of laughing. She began to delight in her own private jokes, whether other people understood them or not. She began to enjoy making things as a child might make them, unambitious and unpretentious, inspired by nothing but the moment.

When Carlotta and Jonathan now came to dinner, Helen was no longer ashamed, and took them to the studio to see her latest fantasies. Carlotta was always imaginative and always truthful. When she liked something she laughed spontaneously, and this gave her the right to be critical, to point out why some things didn't succeed. She was very articulate, and could always justify her feelings.

Helen was impressed: she knew she could not give such sophisticated advice with so light a hand.

Their lives continued much as usual. To others it may have been evident that a certain malaise had come between them, but Helen was unaware of this. Plunged into her own idea of loyalty she could not see why anything should go wrong. Her own feelings seemed to her clear enough, and she could not imagine that theirs might be different. So when Carlotta and Jonathan proposed to her that she should go with them to Barcelona for a new show of Jonathan's work she accepted with pleasure.

For practical reasons Jonathan went on ahead while Helen and Carlotta followed in Helen's car. They started early, stopping on the way on an arid, sandy bank for a picnic. Their meal was a washout – something vague and unmentionable seemed to have come between them. Carlotta sat, morose and gloomy, and Helen's pleasure melted like an ice cream in a warm corner.

That evening they went to the gallery where Jonathan's exhibition was being held. Everything was in confusion, Jonathan was wandering round preoccupied, too busy to notice them. Carlotta seemed to understand what was going on; but this was all Helen ever saw of the show, since she was not invited to the private view a couple of days later. Carlotta and Jonathan seemed apathetic, and

Helen soon found that she was expected to spend a lot of time alone. So she wandered, did some shopping and ate one or two good meals alone.

A few days passed, and Helen had no idea of the arrangements for going home. In the end it was decided they would all leave together in her car, since Jonathan had originally flown from Marseille and left his own at the airport. They set off, Jonathan driving. Helen sat in the back for once, from where she had a good view of Carlotta's head leaning towards Jonathan, intimate and exclusive, telling him something about an American artist whose work she admired, similar to what she wanted to do herself. She described the artworks in detail with an eagerness that impressed Helen with its dream-like fervour and humility in favour of another artist's discoveries. Carlotta invoked the blessing of her erstwhile teacher in America, whom she always referred to as her 'teacher' as though he had taught her mathematics. Helen listened with sympathetic curiosity, although at the time she understood little of what Carlotta described.

It was late when they arrived at the airport. Jonathan stopped at the entrance to the car park, handed over Helen's car, and gave her directions as to the road she should take. They said goodbye with a relief that Helen was in no state to question. It was not only that she was immensely tired but she had no idea what had happened, no clue to explain this unknown state of being. They had reached this desert-like country without any idea of how they had got there. Too worn out to think about it she put it behind her and supposed it was something that would change with time. She took several days to recover from the trip and left Carlotta and Jonathan to do the same.

It must have been about this time that Helen learned that they were serious about selling their house and going to live elsewhere. They had made several excursions to Marseille together, and Helen and Jonathan had indulged in dreams of living in one of those vast warehouses that sit on the quay-side of the commercial port. The buildings all seemed to be empty, and the impression they got was of some monstrous, grand idea dying a slow death, waiting for the reprieve that never came. There were rows of windows, inside which they could imagine huge spaces, ready for experiment. Carlotta, Helen noticed, kept quiet. She did not share such fantasies, feeling probably that reality would have its way in the end. And then Helen heard – she could not, strangely enough, remember how – that they had succeeded in selling their house, even in the then depressed condition of the market, to some well-to-do acquaintance, and were planning to move to Marseille.

Suddenly things seemed to be moving with a new rhythm, at a different speed. Helen, still groping in the dark, felt very out of touch with Carlotta and, still more so, with Jonathan. Dreams of sharing the same warehouse were quite forgotten – and when asked, she had the sense to say she couldn't now think of moving to Marseille. Ten years ago she might have – but not now. She felt, for once, that she had said the right thing, and was secretly pleased with herself. But she also knew that she was slipping back into that state of loneliness from which, three or four years ago, Carlotta and Jonathan had rescued her. What other friends had she whom she could confide in or, at the very least, gossip with? So, feeling lost, she did nothing. And this, she could dimly see, suited them perfectly well.

And then one day she got a letter. It was from Carlotta, and started: 'Helen, dear Helen . . .' and went on to apologise for their neglect of a friend just at a moment when they might have been of some use. How happy they had been to get to know her, how much they had done together that had been enjoyable. But also how soon it became evident to her that it had been Jonathan who had attracted Helen and not Carlotta. Carlotta had done her utmost to put herself into the background and make room for Jonathan and Helen to see more of each other. She would even ask him to call Helen instead of doing it herself, because she knew it would give Helen pleasure. She hoped that, eventually, Helen would learn to appreciate her for what she had to give, alluding to herself as 'deep' and, possibly, boring. Carlotta went on to say that, having waited in vain for such a development, she was no longer prepared to continue 'just sharing' Jonathan and she felt empty, completely empty. She hadn't the energy to go on living in this way, giving all and receiving nothing. Owing to her exhaustion she had stopped recently giving time to other friends as well. She found she was always giving and never receiving. She added that she had been distressed for a long time by Helen's lack of interest in her, but in the end could only accept it. She had loved her deeply – but now felt it was time to put an end to the relationship.

The bomb had exploded. Helen wrote in her diary, which she kept intermittently: 'Something slips from underfoot, turns round and hits you. The world has changed and become bitter and lonely once again. I chew over C's letter – over and over – and I blame myself. But what for exactly? I am not less fond of her than I was, and I can remember no time when I behaved differently or unsympathetically towards her. I go from acute pain, almost physical, to momentary indifference, caused by fatigue. I have replied – but can't see her taking any notice. Her pride has been hurt – or so she thinks – and she is unbelievably obstinate. Will she write me off as a spoiled, insensitive Englishwoman?

'The unfortunate thing is that I haven't been able to go and see her, owing to my wrist. I dreamed that I was embracing her, that I had my arms round her – and I do really love her. How, how has this happened? It is like the moment I broke my wrist – the shock of falling on the floor – I didn't at first know why. It was as though some missile had hit me.'

The shock was certainly great. But Carlotta's answer was, characteristically, analytical and not, she hoped, evasive. 'What made me saddest in your letter,' she wrote, 'is the realisation that I have in some way failed you personally.' Helen replied that 'my feelings for J, though very sweet to me, were childish. Indulged in because I knew it was the last time I would ever feel like that. By being more objective I could have overcome them, but was too lazy to do so. If I have made you feel that I don't appreciate you, I regret it more than I can say, but I find it almost impossible to believe. I love being with you, listening to you, watching you – I enjoy your company – and I do not equate your company with boredom. I am never bored by you although, perhaps because of my own natural optimism (i.e. superficiality), I am sometimes made impatient with what seems a desire to be depressed. Having had a good deal of depression in my life I do not want to take on any extra that can be avoided. At the same time, I always listen to you, I respect your judgement and feelings too much not to. Everything you do is done with grace, spirit and style. You are a wonderful person, and when you say I have not appreciated you, I can only think you have misunderstood me. If my feelings for J are tinged with romantic folly, mine for you are much more solid and durable. If I have not conveyed this, please forgive me. Do not let this be the end of an unexpectedly wonderful relationship – the sort of friendship I never expected to have again.'

And Helen continued: 'I do not know if you have any idea of how lonely I was when you first came into my life, nor how bowled over I was by both of you, Jonathan in a way less than you because he scared me. I felt as though he would break if I touched him – and it was a mistake to allow such a feeling to continue, because it bred a false relationship. But one of the things I loved most was that you were a couple. It's so rare to find two people who have mastered the art of living together and who continue to be intimate and fond of each other. When, eventually, I realised that you had problems it made me very unhappy. It may have been unrealistic to imagine you wouldn't have, but it was at least a generous hope, and it was disturbing and upsetting to realise how much you were suffering. I loved you as a family. I did not come only to see Jonathan, but because you offered me a vision of intelligent, sensitive living, something that was your creation rather than his. Sitting with you in the garden or at the table I felt privileged as though I were a member of the family – Pierre too played his part in all this.'

When her wrist was almost healed, Helen spent a week in England and returned feeling a little better, but still not willing to accept the end of the friendship. There was still no answer from Carlotta, and Helen became haunted by the idea that she would never reply. And if, as she thought, Carlotta had made a definitive decision and only wanted the end of their friendship then what good would a letter do?

Again in her diary she wrote: 'I think of Carlotta all day long. She has shattered something – perhaps my belief in myself as a friend? Is it true that I have been unappreciative of her? Or is it possible that she, having got herself into a false position with regard to me, has seen me in a distorting mirror? Perhaps I have the right to say, How much have you hurt me? I build up this convincing picture in my mind of someone so dignified, so generous and so hurt by my behaviour that she will never reconsider her decision. I cannot imagine her going back on it, even if I go and plead with her. And then there is Jonathan. He has made no sign to me, and although I know he is busy and at bottom probably indifferent to me, I find this strange.

'Then I went, the day before yesterday, to see Carlotta in her flat in Marseille. The intense part of our conversation must have lasted about an hour. In it I admitted that, during our entire friendship, I had been manipulating both her and Jonathan, in order to be loved. I apologised. I listened to all she had to say. Her dignity, her naturalness and the way she had everything laid out in her own mind, was impressive. Her maturity made me feel like a child of ten, and as I listened to her I became more and more unsure of myself until I hardly existed.'

The room they were in was white and, it seemed, everything in it was white – the cups, the saucers, the tablecloth, the walls . . . What did it mean, this holding herself apart, this refusal to participate, and this purity? Was it the purity of love, or the purity of judgement? When Helen asked Carlotta why she had told her she did not appreciate her, Carlotta said that, because of her weak health, she had to be very careful not to expose herself to too much strain. Helen had to confess this had not been clear to her – Carlotta must have hidden it too well. Helen had imagined it had been her evident lack of sympathy for Carlotta's painting that had upset her. But she did not once mention this. Neither did Carlotta say anything that led Helen to think she was jealous of her feelings for Jonathan. Helen asked her how she could sacrifice their friendship to the mere idea that Helen didn't love her enough? In answer she gave Helen the spiel about her health. It was as though you couldn't be ill and have a friend at the same time. Jonathan's opinion was that Helen either didn't do enough or that she went too far . . . he was apparently very critical of her behaviour to Carlotta – but about this she wasn't very explicit. Helen had undertaken a journey to the North Pole – and on the way she found herself turning to ice.

It was an amazingly painful hour spent in this claustrophobic, white apartment, in the tiny room they used as a studio, with some of their newest sketches and drawings pinned to the wall. Showing Helen these, Carlotta was at pains to describe her new and close relationship to Jonathan. They were working on a show to be given in Marseille, and were exploring new avenues of – Helen had forgotten the word – perhaps it was 'research'. They were experimenting with colour – something that before had been absent from what they did, Jonathan's work being black and white, Carlotta's blue and white. Now there was red and, if Helen remembered rightly, green. Their single-minded seriousness, so different from her own slapping on of all and every colour, impressed her. She did her best to understand something that was, in spite of everything, alien to her.

But when she left, after saying a word to Pierre, ill in bed in the next room, her heart felt frozen. The diary went on: 'It became mysteriously, woundingly clear to me

285

that she is not fond of me – in spite of saying to me at one point: "I like you better than anyone else I know." But she made no concessions, she remained distant and cool. Am I to understand that these are her real feelings or the result of her bad health? I embraced her – and then wished I hadn't. At the last minute she said I had not understood her letter – and this gave me a shock. Had I ever understood anything, even in this miraculously clear air? Was I being blind or stupid, or was she hiding something? I left with the impression that quite a lot remained to be said. But should it have been said by me, or her?'

Christmas was an upside-down affair. Usually what Helen enjoyed most was the lack of pressure, the airy solitude, the opportunity to work uninterrupted and to go for walks in the surprisingly warm December sun, seeing a buzzard wheeling against the sky or a perspective of pale blue mountains suggesting the infinite distances of Europe extending over half the world to Russia and beyond. This year however these perceptions were clouded. Luckily her state of mind was not depressed, but rather uneasy, restless and self-questioning. Passive occupations, which she normally enjoyed, all became impossible – a waste of time. And time itself became a torture – each day was too long or too short, too bright in the morning and too dark when the cold evening drew in and forced her to sit by her stove trying to pretend that everything was as it should be.

Christmas over, Helen waited. She could do nothing else. Left alone with herself she tried hard to see further, to come to terms of some sort with what was tormenting her. If she got almost nowhere it was not for lack of effort. Knowing this, she felt she deserved better treatment. But she had to wait until 9 or 10 January before she got another letter from Carlotta. She opened it with a sinking heart, knowing she was going to suffer.

This time it was in French, and began with the avowal that Carlotta hardly knew how to reply to the letters – perhaps two or three – that Helen had not been able to resist sending her. 'Each of us', she wrote, 'floats in a mass of variable emotions or relationships without being able to control them. We often do not really understand what is happening, and often act without explanation. Perhaps what I should have done was to do what is generally done in such circumstances, to refuse further invitations until, slowly, it would have become clear that things had changed, without my intervention. Now, with you [and she used '*vous*' and not '*tu*', Helen noticed] I chose to be completely clear about my feelings because of my respect for you, and I hoped therefore for a certain amount of understanding. No doubt my compassion was not enough, or was not seen as such by you. I neither want to nor can retract anything, and so must repeat as shortly as possible the two things I see as essential, and which I have tried to make plain to you.

'The first thing is my deception at not seeing any growth or development in your personal interest for me. The relation was a false one. Instead of becoming more intimate, you eluded my appeal. I felt myself to be a "convenience" – and it is true I played this game with the utmost skill! When I tried to stop and see whether you would listen to me, I found you paid me no more attention, even though I really needed the reassurance. In a sense I behaved very stupidly – on my own account.

'The second thing can be explained by the strange vagaries of my bad health, which meant that I could no longer bear the pain of being rejected or at the very least held at a distance, while being more or less taken advantage of. Sometimes more, sometimes less. For this reason I needed to write and express my pain at such treatment. In spite of my bad French and long sentences, I think I have now made this clear enough to exclude all other interpretations.

'I could also put things another way: my heart was wounded because not listened to, and I found it hard to accept the painful fact that I was not "promoted" to the greater privilege of exchange and attention which I so needed.

'No one can resent such a lack of sympathy. Perhaps the fault was always my own since I was unable to arouse your interest as I longed to. It would be senseless to want so much from one person, and I must withdraw for a time in order to appreciate one day such limited friendship as you can offer, without asking for something more. Will you come and see me over the Easter holiday? Carlotta.'

Helen wrote in her diary: 'I think of my faults: when I fall short of perfection I cannot accept it. I brush my failure to one side. I "forget" what happened. I expect an exception to be made for me. If I do harm it's by mistake. I am as spoiled as I was as a child. With J and C, I behaved, in spite of being aware of the danger, like a rich protector or patron – and patronised them. Despite being over-sensitive myself, I was not so with them; forty years older than Jonathan and thirty more than Carlotta, I behaved as though I were their contemporary, and became ashamed of myself for my inability to accept the truth. There was, of course, some good in our relationship but, as I said to Carlotta, I had devalued it by trying to manipulate them into loving me because – of all things – I had more money than they had.

'If I were more sure of myself would I feel so anguished? The night before last I woke up at 3 a.m. feeling I had thrown away the only thing in my life that was of any value. The iron entering the soul was an accurate description of my state of mind.

'But the recognition of my own failure calmed me. How meaningless to think in terms of perfection! I shall never know exactly what Carlotta thinks. We are foreign to each other in nationality, in temperament and education. It is too easy for me to idealise her. She is more intelligent, more realistic than I am and has a capacity for seeing herself as others see her which, it is said, allows one to love. She is plunged into a kind of boiling reality, which I shall never know – she faces up to things and does not tell herself lies. And in her art she has the strength to go on doing what she wants to do without a sign of appreciation. Is this passion or blindness, obsessional or visionary? Her painting, so private, suggests the austerity of mathematics or an abstruse theoretical problem stated and re-stated uncompromisingly which, one could say, repels understanding. If perhaps it has a cold splendour, then there is nothing superficially attractive about it.'

Time passed. But the pain did not. Helen thought of Carlotta all day long. She would write in her diary to try to understand her own emotions: 'My vision of Carlotta is of someone with very firm values, very sure of what she thinks and believes. God knows, I don't want her to be otherwise, but I know also that she suffers from depression, from melancholy and from dark, ill-defined fears that take the form of ghosts. Also I shall never forget seeing her here one evening, disappointed about something – I wish I could remember what – repeating something over and over again, her head on Jonathan's shoulder, in a kind of stubborn despair. She wouldn't listen to any word of comfort, either his or mine which, I suppose, were inevitably beside the point for her. I got the impression of someone not only at the bottom of the well, but somehow determined to be there and to stay there. And sometimes she says depressing, gloomy, self-deprecating things in the course of ordinary conversation, such as remarking that she is old and uninteresting next to Jonathan's youth and beauty. All this is horribly, miserably complicated. But how is one to know what the truth is?'

Helen blamed herself, and yet, in spite of her contrition for what she supposed to be her insensitivity, she didn't – or rather couldn't – believe she was responsible for everything. Carlotta's attitude – distant and unresponsive – reduced her to a quivering jelly. Helen was only capable of saying that she had loved, and should therefore be forgiven and, as she came to see weakly enough, all she wanted was forgiveness. She dimly realised that she was responding to a manipulation of a different order from her own, and that Carlotta was in desperate need of honesty and security.

It never occurred to Helen that, quite simply, Carlotta had been jealous. For one thing, Carlotta would never admit it to herself or Helen, nor give any indication that this was the cause of her misery and anger. And Helen, though ashamed of her feelings for Jonathan, knew – if she were honest with herself – that it was little more than calf-love. She saw that a love such as hers could only go so far and no further; and Jonathan's own attitude, his ambiguity and skill, eluded any more intimate contact. But when Helen thought more about it, she realised that Jonathan had undoubtedly responded to her presence. She had been bowled over by his beauty, his wit and his intelligence, but she did not think she had flirted with him. She had been too old, and had fallen for him as a young girl might fall, without any attempt at sophisticated seduction. To start with she had felt an almost too great respect for his art, a feeling that might have easily come between them. But his response to her sympathy, for what he was trying to do, overcame this.

Now it occurred to Helen to ask: if jealousy was not the cause, why had this so upset Carlotta? There are alas other causes of jealousy besides sexual ones. And Helen had, either crudely or insensitively, never thought of such a thing. Had she trod on the path that angels so carefully avoid, and shown more imaginative sympathy with Jonathan than Carlotta could tolerate? What induced Helen

292

to embark on such a line of thought was the fact that she
never felt she was being told the complete truth by Carlotta,
who remained unalterably reserved, and had chosen to fall
back on her weak health as an explanation, rather than
come clean. Why for instance had she never responded to
any of the affectionate things that Helen had both written
and said to her? Were Helen's letters so unconvincing? Did
her affection and admiration, often expressed in an effort
to soften Carlotta's implacability, seem so hypocritical as
not to elicit a single remark or sign of appreciation? As
Helen thought more and more about it she came to the
conclusion that there was a certain inhumanity about
Carlotta's attitude. Surely any honest person would have
been willing to discuss the situation, the impasse they
seemed to have reached? She imagined that it was this
inability to talk about it that made Carlotta feel 'empty'
and exhausted, since what is more exhausting than trying
to hide your true feelings, even from yourself? And jealousy unavowed could easily leave behind it a feeling of
dreadful emptiness; if Carlotta could not admit jealousy
of Jonathan's feelings for Helen, what could be more
exhausting? This, thought Helen, could well be the solution to the whole riddle. Even if the situation was partly
her fault, it was obvious that her own behaviour had been
neither premeditated nor malicious. There was no actual
reason she should not fall in love – everyone knew it was

an involuntary state of mind, and in this case she felt that it had been exonerated by its transparency. Carlotta, spotting it as soon as she did, had at least known all there was to know – and, or rather but, had not been able to cope with it. This realisation staggered Helen, who had always assumed that Carlotta was exactly what she appeared to be – a happy and attractive woman, fulfilled in her art and her relationship with Jonathan even if, for various reasons, she could not talk about it.

Helen realised that there were things that Carlotta, in spite of her depth and intelligence, did not understand. Helen's feelings for Jonathan were coloured by her own very English mind – full of clouds and irrelevancies – and, clear enough to Helen herself, but possibly not to Carlotta, the unnatural gap between Helen's actual age and her experience of life. Sexually, she had had very few experiences: she remembered once, at the ill-chosen moment of crossing a street in Marseille, Carlotta had asked her: 'Didn't you have any lovers all that time after your marriage?' Taken by surprise, Helen admitted as much and Carlotta, interrupted by the traffic, had not pursued the subject. Whereas Helen knew from other conversations that Carlotta, in the freedom of America, had not been so inhibited. She had enjoyed her liberty to the full and had doubtless learned a lot about other people in general, but particularly about men, which had given her the assurance that supported her in spite of her unhappiness – an assurance that Helen found so lacking in herself. Here she was, an old woman, yet as colourless as virgin snow.

Helen had come to the conclusion, after all these years, that it is only possible to give, and to accept help, if love is there too. She doubted if Carlotta ever loved her. She was immensely kind and generous and they often had intimate conversations in which they talked to some extent of themselves. Helen learned a lot about her and came to admire her. But love of this kind is extremely rare and was Helen both egocentric and arrogant, incapable of feeling it? And yet she thought she wanted to help Carlotta – or was this simply a further confirmation of her arrogance? Carlotta must have sensed this. She was too sincere to allow false pride to dominate her, and never actually denied Helen's proffered help or advice, but if she accepted it, this was only after close scrutiny, the results of which she more or less kept to herself. Helen was aware of it, however, and it increased her respect for Carlotta. At the same time, Helen began to realise that, so different were they in temperament, she often found it impossible to understand Carlotta's reactions. Whereas Helen was cold and cerebral, Carlotta was deeply emotional and extremely intelligent. She had a sort of dogged determination, what

Helen could only call a sense of being herself, which enabled her to resist, as the rock resists the inroads of the sea, and to remain finally with her head above water. If anyone could have helped Carlotta it should have been Jonathan but, kind though he was, he seemed incapable of uttering words that held any significance for her.

It wasn't long before Helen heard that Jonathan and Carlotta had left the district to go and live somewhere further south or further west – she did not at first know where – but it was at a considerable distance.

Living alone again, Helen was faced with her own reflection, and did not much like what she saw. When she thought over the past it was in an attempt to put order into it, to clear it up, as though it were a patch of rampant weeds that obscured the truth. Her mind reached back, and she saw through the brambles what she had not been prepared to see at the time. How was it that, even after reading Carlotta's letter, a letter that was so lovingly simple, direct, honest and mature, Helen had remained deaf to her appeal? Whatever the truth of the matter Helen realised that she had failed someone she so much admired. She questioned herself and her state of mind continually yet, for the moment, found it impossible to come up with an answer.